# RAISING RUFUS

# RAISING RUFUS

## DAVID FULK

delacorte press

Text copyright © 2015 by David Fulk
Jacket art copyright © 2015 by Erwin Madrid

All rights reserved. Published in the United States by Delacorte Press, an imprint of Random House Children's Books, a division of Random House LLC, a Penguin Random House Company, New York.

Delacorte Press is a registered trademark and the colophon is a trademark of Random House LLC.

Visit us on the Web! randomhousekids.com

Educators and librarians, for a variety of teaching tools, visit us at RHTeachersLibrarians.com

*Library of Congress Cataloging-in-Publication Data*
Fulk, David.
Raising Rufus / David Fulk. — First edition.
pages cm
Summary: "A lonely 11-year-old science nerd named Martin discovers an ancient egg and soon finds himself 'surrogate mom' to a very outlandish pet—a T. rex. But when his secret gets too big to keep from the world, Martin must find his inner hero to save the one thing he's come to really care about"—Provided by publisher.
ISBN 978-0-385-74464-5 (hc) — ISBN 978-0-375-99178-3 (glb) —
ISBN 978-0-385-39072-9 (ebook)
[1. Tyrannosaurus rex—Fiction. 2. Dinosaurs—Fiction.] I. Title.
PZ7.F95157Rai 2015
[Fic]—dc23
2014009799

The text of this book is set in 12-point Century Schoolbook.
Book design by Trish Parcell

Printed in the United States of America
10 9 8 7 6 5 4 3 2 1
First Edition

For Marie and Neal

# ONE

**T**he hunter would not be denied.

His spear drawn and ready, he crashed his way over, under, around, and through the bushes and brambles in his path. His arms and legs were getting mightily scratched up, but that wouldn't slow him down, not today. He focused on his fleeing prey with a big cat's intensity, determined that it would not escape. He was, after all, the king of the forest, the Master Huntsman.

Of course, Martin wasn't really a Masai tribesman with a spear; he was an eleven-year-old kid with a bug net. And his prey was no swift and nimble antelope; it was a black swallowtail butterfly. But somehow the chase was more fun if he let his imagination fly a bit.

Besides, he really needed that swallowtail for his collection. So he summoned his inner warrior and charged after the fluttering bug as it led him deeper and deeper into the woods, a good quarter mile beyond his usual hiking range.

"Come on, *land*," he commanded through clenched teeth. "You know you have to!"

He wasn't supposed to stray that far from the path, but the longer the chase went on, the more determined he was to make his catch. So, when the crafty butterfly found its way to the Kinnewoc limestone quarry and headed down the ramp, Martin didn't slow down to read the sign on the traffic gate:

**DANGER!**
**ROCKSLIDE AREA**
**KEEP OUT**

He slid underneath the gate and sprinted down the steep dirt roadway, following the darting, dodging insect all the way to the bottom of the quarry. The work crews were gone, and they had taken all their trucks and digging machines with them. So there was nothing blocking the way as Martin chased his six-legged prey across the quarry floor. He was huffing and wheezing, exhausted by the long chase, and now, for the first time, he couldn't escape the thought that the

Master Huntsman might just have to go home, get a sandwich, and try again some other time.

Then, silently, almost right in front of him, the butterfly circled in and made a slow, graceful landing on a clump of rock sticking out from the wall. His focus revived, Martin raised his net and tiptoed forward. The swallowtail slowly opened and closed its wings, the black-and-yellow scales glistening in the sunlight.

*Closer . . . closer . . . that's it, hold steady . . .*

The instant Martin got within striking range, *whoosh-whap!* He smacked the net against the wall.

But this day would belong to the hunted, not the hunter. The butterfly slipped away just in the nick of time, and all Martin could do was watch as it spiraled straight up, up, up, and over the quarry wall, free to flit among the trees and torment other young bug hunters for the rest of its days.

*"Aaaaaaaaach,"* Martin groaned. "How could you be that quick?"

But his disappointment quickly vanished; now an oddly bright glimmer in the wall caught his attention. What was all that *ice* doing mixed in with the rocks? It seemed to be melting quickly in the sun—water was dripping down across the whole length of the rock face. And what kind of rocks were those? Limestone, right, but other kinds were mixed in with the ice, strange ones he couldn't remember ever seeing before—and he considered himself something of a rock expert.

Martin touched the cold, wet surface of the wall, and a small chunk fell off. He picked it up and brought it close to his face, rubbing his thumb across the flat surface. No, this was definitely not an ordinary piece of limestone. Right there on the smooth face of the stone was the clear outline of . . . what? A bird's foot? Maybe, or maybe not, but it was definitely something that was alive once—and a long, *long* time ago.

"Wow. A fossil!"

Martin had seen pictures of fossils before, but he never imagined he would find one just a twenty-minute hike from his own backyard. The quarrymen must have dug straight into an ancient dying ground for creatures that lived millions of years ago.

As he reached over his shoulder and dropped the fossil into his backpack, all thoughts of hunters and antelopes and butterflies disappeared from Martin's head. If there was one fossil here, there could be *hundreds.* Imagine being the only kid in this corner of Wisconsin with his own, personally gathered fossil collection!

Fascinated, he reached for the wall again. But the instant his hand touched it, another rock came loose—a bigger one, higher up. Martin flinched as it hit the ground behind him with a loud *thud.* Then came a sharp *crackle,* and he had to duck and cover his head as more rocks rained down around him.

*That's it—I'm out of here!*

He spun on his heel to make a dash away from the rock face. But before he could take a second step, there was a tremendous RUMBLE and a giant slab of rock came crashing down from the wall, blocking his way. He gave a loud grunt and took a big hop backward, trying to keep his balance. Then, before he could even think about where to go next, there was an even bigger *rumble* and *crash,* and the very ground under his feet gave way!

"Holy mama!" he yowled, and he squeezed his eyes shut as he suddenly felt himself dropping straight down as though a trapdoor had opened up right underneath him, and rocks and boulders and chunks of ice came thundering down, completely burying the spot where he had been standing only a few brief seconds ago.

Then . . . silence.

Anybody watching what had just happened would definitely think that was the end of Martin Tinker. But as it turned out, that swallowtail was not the only one having a lucky day. Underneath all those rocks and ice chunks, below ground level, there was one really, really small open space—and Martin somehow had managed to end up inside it.

*"Wow,"* he whispered. "Am I still alive?"

It was just about pitch-black in there, but he was able to move around a little—one of the few times, he realized, when it was actually a good thing to be skinny.

As he took a few long, deep breaths to help settle his nerves, he suddenly remembered something. The other day they'd said on the TV news that the

Kinnewoc crew had accidentally drilled into a vein of dark ice, so now the quarry wall was unstable. It wasn't safe to work on, and the quarry would be shut down.

Martin felt like kicking himself for not thinking of that before he went charging down there—but he could barely move, so any kicking was out of the question.

*Okay, don't panic,* he thought. *You can get out of this . . .*

He awkwardly reached around behind his back and unzipped his backpack. It took a good half minute or so of groping, but he finally got his hand around his cell phone. And when he pressed the switch with his thumb and the screen lit up, he felt a surge of relief.

First he reached over with the phone light to check out a nasty scrape on his elbow—by some crazy stroke of luck, his only real injury from the fall. Then, hands shaking, he shined the light around his rocky cubbyhole. He could see a crack of daylight through a narrow chute above; with determination and a little luck, a short crawl should get him up and out.

"All right . . . okay. I've got this . . ."

As he clamped his lips tight and got set to start crawling, he could see in the dim light that there were even more of those mysterious fossils all around him. Even though he knew it was probably not the smartest thing to do just now, he couldn't resist the urge to pick up a few of the smaller ones and slip them into his backpack—no easy maneuver when you're stuck in a rocky, icy space not much bigger than the trunk of a Buick.

When he had gathered a few handfuls of the fossils, Martin decided he'd better not mess around any longer, and began his uncomfortable crawl toward the opening above. He slithered his way along, holding his breath as he carefully navigated the jagged rock edges. Then, when he was halfway there . . . his knee banged on something cold.

*"Ow!"*

He reached down with the glowing phone and saw that he had bumped something very odd—a smooth, oval object, a bit smaller than a football, grayish-brown and covered with . . . were those speckles, or just chunks of dirt? Hard to tell, because half of the thing was covered with ice, and the other half had a crust of grit and hard clay stuck to it. Martin edged backward a few inches to get a closer look. If this was a fossil, it was nothing at all like the others.

Another *rumble* in the rocks above sent a new shot of jitter juice surging through his stomach. With no time to wrangle the heavy object into his backpack, he quickly scooped it up with his left hand, tucked it tight against his rib cage, and scrambled the rest of the way up to the narrow opening—and, with one last big push, popped out into the open air. Freedom!

Stooped over from the weight in his hand, he sprinted away from the wall as fast as his spindly legs would carry him. And his escape came not a moment too soon, because now there was an enormous

CRASH, and suddenly the whole quarry wall gave way, cascading down in an avalanche of rocks and ice—and totally obliterating the small crevasse he had been trapped inside only seconds before.

Having made it a safe distance away, he straightened up and turned to watch the spectacular scene, slack-jawed and wide-eyed. He stood there, his heart thumping, hacking and coughing from the tons of dust, until all the rocks had finally settled. *So that's what it's like to almost die,* he thought. Then he thought of what his mom and dad might do if they ever found out how close he had come to an early grave. So of course, they would never hear a thing about it.

Realizing his fingers and left side were starting to feel numb, Martin looked down at the frozen stone he had forgotten he was holding. He brushed away some frost and dust, held it to his ear, knocked on it lightly, took a sniff—but it was not a thing that would give up its secrets easily.

He knew what he would do: take it home, set it up in his backyard barn lab, and get going on some serious research.

What he didn't know was that this strange, cold stone was going to change his life forever.

# TWO

*R*eep *reep deedy bip!*

The ringtone wasn't that loud, but Martin was so deep in concentration that it made him jump a little. He reached across his workbench and grabbed the phone.

"Hi, Mom."

"Martin, do you have my cheese grater?"

"Um . . . yeah." He had the grater, all right. He'd been using it to scrape at the grit and grime that was stuck to that egg-shaped stone he'd found in the quarry.

"What are you using it for?"

"You know. Stuff."

"Honey, I need it back. I'm doing one of those cheesy-noodle things you like."

Actually, Martin didn't much care for the cheesy-noodle thing. But he didn't feel like arguing the point. "Okay."

"Listen, your dad called from work and he can't find his truck keys. Would you be a star and bike over there with the spare set?"

"Oh, um—"

"You're the best, monkey-bean. And bring my grater before you go."

Martin was trying to think of an excuse not to go, but he wasn't quick enough; she was gone. So he took a deep breath, rubbed his eyes, and geared up to venture out of the lab and face the world.

It wasn't an actual *lab,* of course, with test tubes and weird equipment and that sort of thing. But it definitely worked for Martin's purposes. The land that his family's house was on had once been part of a small dairy farm, and though the house itself was fairly ordinary by Menominee Springs standards, the backyard was huge, and there was a big stone barn at the far end. The good thing for Martin was that his parents never used the barn for anything more than a giant storage space, so he had talked them into letting him use a corner of it for his own private science lab.

And he spent a *lot* of time in that lab. Not having any real friends to speak of, he hung out in there pretty much every day after school, and on weekends, too. The lab was where he got to hang with some *real* friends—friends who always listened to him, who never snubbed him or made fun of him, who were there to support him when things got him down.

True, these friends tended to be not exactly *living*—collections of stones, dried leaves, and dead bugs, all neatly arranged on shelves and in display boxes. But Martin looked forward to hanging out with them every day and, naturally, adding to their numbers on a regular basis. He even had names for his favorite pals, like the perfectly preserved cecropia moth he called Gigundo because it was so—well, *gigundo,* and a brilliant purple piece of quartz he called Charlie, though he wasn't sure exactly why.

The other great thing about the barn was that the door was only a few steps from the edge of the woods, which conveniently started right where the Tinkers' yard ended. So, on a typical spring day like today, Martin could come straight home from school, make a quick stop in the house to grab a snack, hustle on out to the barn to pick up his bug net and assorted gear, and head right out into the pine groves for a new day of discovery and adventure. Out there he might catch a few interesting bugs, dig up one or two new rock specimens, maybe skip stones across a pond for a while, sit on a rock and leaf through a good bug book—and never have to cross paths with another human being.

His mom worked in the public library in the afternoons and didn't like the idea of Martin wandering out there alone among the bugs and badgers and bears and lord-knows-what. But his dad had convinced her that it was healthy for Martin to exercise a little independence, so they decided to let him go—as long as he knew the full rules of the road, which she quizzed him on regularly.

"How many leaves on a poison ivy twig?"

"Three."

"You can touch stream water, but . . ."

"Don't drink it."

"What if it looks like rain?"

"Come right home."

"And if you see a bear . . ."

"Back away slowly, don't make eye contact, and call nine-one-one. Then start singing, because they hate that."

Nobody had ever seen a bear in that part of the woods, but it made no difference to Mrs. Tinker; she wanted Martin to be totally prepared for anything. So she gave him a can of Harlan Ziffer's Bear-Away Spray to carry with him on his hikes—just in case. She also insisted he take a sun hat, a water bottle, a first-aid kit, a banana for energy, a pocket knife, a plastic poncho, an air horn, mosquito repellent, and an extra battery for his phone.

Martin knew his mom meant well, but to him it seemed a bit extreme. It was just way too much stuff to haul around. So he generally made it a point to "forget" to take most of it with him on his nature walks.

Martin was pretty grumpy about having to do this errand, and he was eager to get it over with. He really wanted to get back to his lab to study that big, frozen oval stone, and all those fascinating fossils, too. There was one that looked like part of a spiky flounder, and another one that could have been either a very ugly shrimp or a very hairy spider, before it got flattened forever onto a smooth piece of rock. Martin couldn't wait to study them and learn more, but for now, wait was what he would have to do.

As he pedaled his bike across town, the postcard-pretty surroundings and soft breezes took his mind off his lab work and gave his mood a boost. After all, late April was the best time of year in Menominee Springs: the deep chill of winter was gone, flowers were just starting to bloom, the local fauna were making their summer debut, and the swarms of tourists hadn't yet descended on the town. It seemed like everybody was out and about, and smiles were as plentiful as the bumblebees on the spring daffodils.

Part of the reason everybody was so chipper was that they were looking forward to the many dollars the tourists would soon be bringing to town with them. And nobody looked forward to that more than Mr. Tinker's boss, Ben Fairfield, who was already the richest man in Menominee Springs. He got that way by being the owner of the Trout Palace, a sprawling house of amusements that attracted vacationers from hundreds of miles around. Set on thirty acres of prime wooded parkland, the Trout Palace had, as Mr. Fairfield loved to boast, something for everyone.

Martin rode up and parked his bike next to the big wooden sign at the front gate that said it all:

# WELCOME to the TROUT PALACE

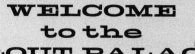

*Northern Wisconsin's ultimate playland for the whole family!*

## HEART O' THE WOODS RESTAURANT
*(Catch your own fish!)*

- *Biggest arcade in the state*
- *Slot-car racing*
- *Water slide*
- *Mini golf*
- *Beaver ballet and muskrat races hourly*
- *Beautiful nature exhibits (so real you'll think you're there!)*
- *Hilarious skits in the Walleye Theater*
- *Funnel cakes, ice cream, and burgers*
- *Exciting rides for the kids*

*And much, much more!*

## Season Opening May 28

Martin went through the gate and walked past the outdoor rides, which hadn't really interested him much since he was about eight—a mini train, a merry-go-round, a slow-speed coaster, pony rides, and a few other unchallenging distractions—and stepped up to the front entrance of the main building.

The Trout Palace was a big half cylinder of corrugated steel that reminded Martin of a hangar for a jumbo jet, if there were a way to get a jumbo jet into the middle of the woods. The inside was laid out so that anywhere you looked, something would draw you in. Everything promised on the sign was there, and more, though none of it was as modern and thrilling as you might expect. Most of the attractions had been there, unchanged, for more than thirty years.

There were a lot of reasons to visit Menominee Springs in the summer—fishing, camping, hiking, waterskiing, or just soaking in the relaxing, woodsy atmosphere—but it was the Trout Palace that really brought people in. There was just something about catching your own lunch in a man-made pond or watching a dancing beaver in a tutu that made folks want to pile their families into the SUV and head across the state. And they kept coming year after year, defying all logic—never mind the video games, the Internet, the big-screen TVs, and all the other modern gadgets that usually occupied people's leisure time.

All of which made Ben Fairfield a very happy man. Or so you might think if you were one of the visitors he would personally greet just inside the entrance with a big smile and a firm handshake, his bald dome glistening under the tube fluorescents.

"Hi there! Welcome to the Trout Palace!" he'd say. "Where're you folks from?"

"La Crosse."

"Oh, yeah. My favorite town." Then he would lean down to the kids. "You ready to have some fun, partners?"

"Uh-huh."

"Well, don't spend all your dad's money. Ha ha ha ha ha!"

Martin didn't much care for Mr. Fairfield—partly because he always called him Murphy, and partly because of the way he treated the Trout Palace employees, which was nothing at all like the way he treated his customers. The people who worked there were mostly high schoolers on summer break, and Mr. Fairfield never missed a chance to throw off a nasty remark or make them feel stupid. Whenever Martin was in the place, he couldn't help feeling sorry for them.

There were a few Trout Palace employees, though, who were treated quite a bit better by Ben Fairfield. These were the ones with a lot of skills and experience, the ones Mr. Fairfield realized he needed as much as they needed him—like the technical supervisor, Mr. Gordon Tinker. Martin's dad was the man who made sure all the electrical and mechanical contraptions were in top working order at all times. He was the best there was, and Mr. Fairfield knew it.

Nobody was busier in the weeks before the Trout Palace opened than Mr. Tinker. So as Martin walked up to the building's grand entryway, he was hoping it wouldn't be too hard to find him. He still had that bizarre frozen fossil on his mind, and he just wanted to pass off the keys and get back home to the lab. Plus, a quick exchange would minimize the chances of running into Mr. Fairfield.

Luckily, just as Martin came in the main door, he ran into his dad—or his dad's legs, actually. He was standing on a ladder with the upper half of his body inside a giant fiberglass fish that hung from wires attached to the ceiling. The fish's gaping mouth had some gear work connected to it, and Mr. Tinker was wrestling with a very stubborn bolt.

"Get loose, you little bugger . . ."

"Hi, Dad. I got your spare keys."

"Huh? . . . Oh, great. Thanks, buddy." He slipped the wrench into his tool belt and got set to come down the ladder. "Y'know, I had those things when I got out of the truck this morning—"

"Hey, Gordo! Think fast!" a voice boomed out.

Martin's dad looked down just in time to see Ben Fairfield fire a football in his direction. Instinctively, he reached through the fish's mouth and made a smooth catch.

Mr. Fairfield grinned impishly. "Still got those great hands."

"Tell it to this bolt."

"Ha haaa! . . . Hey there, Murphy! What's the good word?"

"Hi," Martin mumbled. In his head he was bemoaning his bad luck, but even more than that he felt a little embarrassed for his dad, because he knew that football was kind of a sore point for him. Years ago his "great hands" had made him a star wide receiver on the Menominee Springs High football team. He was so good that he had earned a full scholarship to the University of Wisconsin. But it all came crashing down when a serious knee injury in the last game of his senior year put an end to the scholarship, his college plans, and his dreams of making it to the National Football League. He ended up marrying his hometown sweetheart—Martin's mom—right after high school, and went to work at the Trout Palace.

Luckily, Mr. Fairfield changed the subject. "Come on down. I want to show you guys something."

As Mr. Tinker dislodged himself from the fish and descended the ladder, Martin, hoping for a quick escape, edged backward. "I have to, um . . ."

His dad quickly shook his head and motioned for Martin to follow. They walked with Mr. Fairfield across the Trout Palace floor, past all the busy workers setting up the game booths, concession stands, and nature displays.

"Just came in this morning," Mr. Fairfield said. "This one's gonna pay your outrageous salary all by itself."

Mr. Tinker played along. "I like it already."

Mr. Fairfield forced a short cackle that ended quickly as he spotted one of his young employees painting a few last details on a popcorn booth. "Hey! That thing is sticking out too far. I told you that twenty times already!" As the kid struggled to push the booth into a better spot, Mr. Fairfield muttered, "Numbskull," just a bit too loudly. "Yeah, it's gonna be a big year, Gordo. Our biggest ever. This place'll be busting at the seams."

"You haven't been wrong yet, Ben."

"Hey, genius is a burden, am I right? Ha ha! Okay. You ready for this?"

He grabbed the corner of a large tarpaulin draped over something that looked about as big as the Tinkers' front porch. Then, *swoosh!* He pulled the tarp away to reveal . . . well, Martin wasn't sure exactly what. It was a really big box—a room, kind of—open at one end, with a three-dimensional woodland scene at the back and, at the opening where they stood, a toy rifle mounted on a post. A big, arc-shaped sign over the front announced proudly:

"Geez. Will you look at that," Mr. Tinker said unconvincingly. He and Martin traded sidelong frowns.

"You give the man a dollar . . . and . . ." Mr. Fairfield stepped up to the rifle, pushed a big red button, and took aim as the forest scene sprang to life—papier-mâché deer and bears popping up and down among the trees, creaky plastic ducks taking off from the brush, smiling cutout fish jumping out of a "stream" that was nothing more than a bunch of tinsel blown by a fan.

Mr. Fairfield fired away at the animals as they quickly appeared and disappeared, the fake *boom* of the gun sounding more like a cannon blast than a rifle shot. Mr. Tinker could only scratch his head as Mr. Fairfield's score rapidly mounted on an electronic counter, with a helpful *ding* announcing each hit. Mr. Fairfield was thoroughly absorbed, snickering like a third grader, but as far as Martin was concerned, the demonstration went on way longer than it needed to. All he could think was *How long do I have to keep watching this?*

Thankfully, the show came to an end when the rifle suddenly broke off from its mounting.

"Ah, criminy," Mr. Fairfield muttered. "Anyway, you get the idea."

"What can I say, Ben?" Martin's dad said. "You've done it again."

"U-Bag-Em! They're gonna come all the way from the Twin Cities to play this one. Am I right, Murphy?"

Martin plastered on a fake grin, though he couldn't help thinking that people in the Twin Cities—and everywhere else, for that matter—could get a higher level of entertainment right at home on their Play-Stations and Xboxes.

He was saved from having to say something by the breathless approach of a teenage girl in a yellow T-shirt with TROUT PALACE STAFF emblazoned across the front.

"Mr. Fairfield! One of the beavers got loose and he's in the restaurant."

"So? Catch him."

"We can't find him."

Mr. Fairfield rolled his eyes, then grumbled as he headed off with the girl. "Bunch of helpless babies working here . . ." He made a half turn back to Mr. Tinker. "Fix that gun, will you, pal?"

"Oh, Ben . . ." Martin's dad flipped the football back to Mr. Fairfield.

"Nah, you keep it. Here y'go, Murphy. Go long."

He chucked the ball toward Martin—who ducked out of the way just in time. As the ball bounced down the midway, Mr. Tinker gave him a sour look. Martin looked back at him sheepishly. "I wasn't ready," he lied. They both knew his football skills were pretty much nonexistent. He really did wish he were better at it, but somehow he never could relate to that odd-shaped ball. It was a shape better suited for . . . well, a frozen fossil, for one.

"Here's your keys. See ya." He tossed the keys to his dad and made a quick U-turn.

As Martin scurried off, fervently hoping to avoid what he knew was coming next, his dad went to retrieve the football. "Hey," he called after him. "I'll give you some pointers later. We'll try a new approach. All right, pal?"

"Sure thing, Dad," Martin called back, rounding a corner.

For now, he'd made his escape. But somehow he knew that "Sure thing" would come back to haunt him.

# THREE

**M**elissa Gunders got the first good laugh of the day. All she had to do was stand at the front of the class while her long blond hair slowly rose off her shoulders and stood straight out like a spiky yellow halo. Nothing magical: she had reached this glorified state by resting her hand on a silver ball on top of a thick, cylindrical shaft while Mr. Eckhart, the young science teacher, cranked a handle on its side.

Amid cackles and hoots from the class, Mr. Eckhart let go of the crank and got down to business. "Okay. Who can explain what's going on?"

Everybody had gotten the entertainment value, but obviously not the lesson; no hands went up. Well, actually, there was one hand in the air at the side of the room, near the back. Mr. Eckhart didn't bother to look.

"Anybody besides Martin?"

Martin hated it when he did that. But he understood that Mr. Eckhart was just trying to get everybody else to get their brains out of neutral.

All the class could come up with, though, was blank stares—until the silence was broken by a loud, raspy voice from the fourth row.

"She's holding in a big one."

The laughter started right up again, which drew a self-satisfied smirk from the guy who said it, Donald Grimes. Donald was a stocky kid with a buzz cut and a crooked grin who liked to think of himself as the class comedian. To Martin, though, he was nothing but an annoying jerk who picked on him all the time.

Other kids jumped in with their own theories.

"A bug flew up her nose."

"She's got really bad head lice."

"She's an alien from Uranus!"

Martin rolled his eyes. But for the rest of the class, each wisecrack was good for another round of big laughs, and even Mr. Eckhart grinned a little. "Okay, save it for creative writing class. I need a scientific explanation."

Again, no hands. "All right, Martin," he said with a resigned sigh. "Enlighten us."

Martin spoke in a soft voice, but with no hesitation. "The static charge causes the protons in her body to flow into the ground, leaving a surplus of electrons. Since the electrons repel each other, each strand of hair is pushed away from all the others."

"Bo-o-o-o-o-oring," Donald Grimes hooted.

"It happens to be correct," Mr. Eckhart said. "Better remember it, amigos. It might be on the test." Everybody groaned, but he couldn't hide a tiny smile, and they knew he was only teasing. "Tell you what. No test if anybody can tell me what this is called." He put his hand on the silver thing with the crank.

Not even Martin could come up with that one. All he could think of was how much the silver ball reminded him of that egg-shaped thing back in his lab.

Donald offered his theory: "An electro-zap space blaster."

The class had another good laugh, and Mr. Eckhart squinted at Donald. "Just for that, *two* tests."

Everybody yowled and groaned, but they abruptly went quiet as the door opened and Ms. Olerud, the regular classroom teacher, poked her head into the room. She threw Mr. Eckhart a thin smile, pointing to her watch.

"Once again, science bows to brute authority," he said, picking up his books. "Okay, crew. See you Thursday." He pushed the silver contraption, which was mounted on a little wheeled platform, in front of him as he headed for the door. "Van de Graaff generator," he half whispered to the class, then nodded to Ms. Olerud and disappeared into the hall.

Ms. Olerud had been the sixth-grade teacher for

the past five years, and pretty much everybody liked her. But she was definitely more of a stickler for class-room order than Mr. Eckhart was, so everyone knew they would have to settle down and get back to business now.

"Everybody, you have a new classmate," she said as a freckle-faced girl in a mismatched plaid skirt and purple-striped top followed her into the room, eyes darting around nervously. She had a yellow number 2 pencil behind her ear, and the brightest red hair Martin had ever seen.

"This is Audrey Blanchard," said Ms. Olerud. "She just moved here from . . . Oshkosh? Is that right, Audrey?"

"Yes," Audrey almost whispered.

"Please make her feel welcome. Why don't you sit there, dear?" Ms. Olerud pointed to an empty desk in the fourth row, then turned away to write on the board as Audrey walked stiffly up the aisle. Watching her out of the corner of his eye, Martin could relate to how uncomfortable she obviously was, being stared at by the whole class. If there was one thing worse than being the class geek, it was being the new kid, especially so near the end of the school year.

Just as Audrey sat, somebody—yes, Donald Grimes—broke the silence with a half-covered, goofy-voiced: "Oh look, it's Tippi Tomato!"

The whole class burst out laughing. Tippi Tomato was a funny red-haired character they knew from Saturday-morning cartoons.

Ms. Olerud wheeled around, glaring icicles.

"Who said that?" Her eyes swept sternly across the suddenly innocent faces. "That is very unkind, and we do not do that in this classroom. Understood?" After a thick silence, she quickly got back down to business. "Geography books! Chop-chop."

As everybody dug for their books, Martin snuck one more glimpse at the unfamiliar face in the room. But when Audrey took a sidelong glance right back at him, he quickly looked away. Eye contact? With a *girl*? Not for Martin Tinker.

For the rest of the day, Martin found himself thinking more and more about his big frozen stone. He'd never gotten a chance to get back to it the night before, and now the ball on that Van de Graaff generator had put it at the front of his mind again, and he was eager to get home and start working on it.

But as usual, he also got more and more nervous as the end of the day approached. For Martin, leaving the school building was something to dread, not look forward to.

When the bell rang at 2:50, kids streamed into the schoolyard on their way to the bus or, for the ones like Martin who lived reasonably close by, their homes. For Martin, this meant taking a few extra minutes for some careful planning. If he timed his exit from the building just right, he might be able to avoid an encounter with Donald Grimes, who seemed to have made it the main mission of his life to ruin Martin's.

Donald had been held back a grade, so he was a year older than everybody else, and somehow he felt that made him king of the sixth grade. And to prove it, he went after the easiest target, which was, quite obviously, Martin Tinker. Sometimes, if Donald was feeling especially devilish, he would challenge Martin to a "wrestle," which was really just an excuse to twist his arm, clamp him in a headlock, kick him in the butt, deliver a noogie, spin him around, and pin him on the ground—preferably in a muddy spot. Martin didn't really fight back; for one thing, Donald was stronger than he was, and for another, he knew that if he did, Donald would give him an even worse working over.

Today, though, it seemed like things might go a bit better. When Martin pushed the door partway open and peeked out, he saw Donald and two of his buddies, Nate Stoller and Tyler Braun, chatting in the schoolyard as Donald repeatedly chucked a tennis ball against a wall, catching it on the rebound. It looked to Martin like they would be distracted enough to leave him alone, so he prepared his escape.

As he slipped out the door, he could hear the boys' conversation, which, as usual, was deep and philosophical.

"I'm telling you, man. If you fart, burp, and sneeze all at the same time, you explode."

"Get outta here."

"Absolute truth."

"You're full of it."

"I've seen it happen."

"Where?"

"In the McDonald's parking lot."

"How come I never heard about that?"

"Probably because you're an idiot."

As quietly as possible, Martin started down the steps. But he stopped when, out of the corner of his eye, he saw Audrey Blanchard walking along the building wall toward the gate.

Donald spotted her too. "Hey, Tippi Tomato! Think fast!"

When Audrey turned to look, he reared back and fired the tennis ball. It just missed her head, ricocheting off the wall behind her and bouncing back to Donald, who led his pals in a round of big laughs.

Audrey stood up straight and threw the boys a withering glare. "Very funny."

"Hey, Tippi! Your head's on fire!" Donald hollered, and unleashed another fastball.

Audrey ducked out of the way. "Cut it out, you cretin!" she snapped. She tried to run, but Tyler and Nate, both cackling like chimpanzees, split up and blocked her escape in either direction. Now Donald started peppering her with a barrage of throws. She managed to dodge it each time, but the ball kept bouncing back to him.

"Faster! Think faster!" he squawked as she danced awkwardly, fumbling her books to the ground.

Martin stood frozen at the bottom of the steps, watching. He felt sorry for Audrey, having been in her shoes many times. But he also knew if he tried to do anything about it, the game would turn on him. He took a step away—but stopped when one of Donald's pitches glanced off Audrey's foot, and the ball bounced away and rolled right up to him.

"Throw me the ball, Tinker," Donald said, not smiling.

Martin looked down at the ball at his feet, then slowly stooped and picked it up.

"Tinker, he said throw him the ball!" Tyler snapped.

Martin didn't move. Somehow the command to throw wasn't making it from his brain to his hand.

His hesitation gave Audrey just enough time to scoop up her books and dart out the gate. Caught off guard, the guys could only watch her scurry away.

Donald turned to Martin with a glower, and for what was only a few seconds but seemed like about a minute and a half, they stared at each other. Martin felt his stomach twist into a pretzel. Then—knowing exactly what would come next—he made a break for it. Unfortunately, his backpack full of books was weighing him down, and the others were faster runners anyway, and they headed him off before he could make it to the gate.

"Someplace you gotta be, Tinks?" Nate said with a grin as the three boys surrounded him.

"I could have sworn I said throw the ball," Donald said.

"I heard you say it," Tyler offered.

"Me too," Nate added helpfully.

"So how come Tinker still has it?" said Donald. "He'll have to be punished. Hmmmm . . . what should we do?"

As the boys thought it over, dramatically exaggerating their thinking poses, Martin tried to map out an escape. If he ducked down low and darted between Nate and Tyler, he might be able to make it out the gate and into the bus driver's view before they could catch up to him. But just as he was about to give it a shot, the bus let out a belch of black exhaust and rolled off down the street.

Before Martin could even start on a plan B, Donald's face lit up. "Oh! Y'know what we haven't done in a *long* time, Tinker Bell? We haven't had a good wrestle."

Nate and Tyler gurgled and chuckled with anticipation. Now Martin knew his only hope was negotiation. "Look, Grimes. If I wrestle with you, what happens? You just beat me up like always, and it doesn't prove anything new. Or else somebody catches us, or I get hurt, and then you get in trouble. Or maybe, by some really weird fluke of nature, I beat *you* up, and you have to live with the shame for the rest of your life. So what's the point?"

Donald gaped emptily at Martin, as though somebody had just tried to explain Einstein's theory of general relativity to him. "Gee, Marty," he said, his face a picture of sincerity. "I never thought of it like that. Maybe you're right." The smirks on Tyler's and Nate's faces faded a bit; even they didn't seem quite sure what was going on in Donald's bristly noggin. But Donald put a quick end to that as a big, goofy grin broke out on his face. "OR NOT!"

In a flash, Martin found himself in his least favorite position: stooped over, his head locked in the crook of Donald's arm, being pulled in a tight circle as Donald's knuckles rubbed across his scalp like a buzz saw. Tyler and Nate hooted and chortled, and for good measure threw in a few whacks to Martin's butt every time Donald turned him their way. Martin's face turned a deep crimson, and he was gritting his teeth so hard that it felt like a few of them might crack. The guys weren't really hurting him all that much, at least not physically, but the thought of being at the mercy of these boneheads made him want to scream. He couldn't allow that to happen, though— they would only think they'd won.

Then again, maybe Martin would get lucky today. Out of the corner of his eye, he spotted a sheriff's squad car pulling up just outside the gate. Tyler and Nate backed away from the wrestlers, pretending they had nothing to do with the proceedings, as the sheriff, a guy with a long nose and the beginnings of a potbelly, stepped out of the car and called over.

"Let's go, Donnie boy."

"Okay, Dad. Just a second," Donald called back,

and he yanked Martin up straight and brushed him off, as though he'd just helped him up from a fall.

The sheriff was trying not to smile. "Okay, buddy. Give the little guy a break, eh?"

Yes, that was the sad truth of it: Sheriff Frank Grimes was the father of Martin's tormentor-in-chief.

Donald gave Martin one last "friendly" slap on the back before sauntering off to catch his ride home. As he strutted out the gate and headed for the car, his dad grinned. "You little devil," he said, giving Donald's spiky hair a ruffle. "What are you doing, eh?" He shook his head, chuckling, and the two of them got into the squad car.

As the car headed off down the street, Donald leaned out the window to throw one last smirk and wave at Martin. *If only I could spit venom like a Mangshan pit viper,* Martin thought, *I could wipe that smile off his face for good.*

Tyler and Nate wandered off, and Martin grimly picked up his books and returned them to his backpack. He finished dusting himself off, then looked himself over; at least there weren't any rips or scrapes or bruises to have to explain at home.

He tried his best to take these episodes in stride, though the unfairness of it all really made his blood boil. Why couldn't *his* dad be a policeman who let him do whatever he wanted?

As he zipped up the pack, he caught a glimpse of something across the way: there, standing on the other side of the fence, was Audrey Blanchard, watching him with a vaguely sympathetic expression. But Martin wasn't in the mood for sympathy just now. Knowing she had seen the whole thing only added to his humiliation. He flung the backpack over his shoulder and marched out the gate and down the street, trying to get as far away as possible.

# FOUR

Martin went for a long hike in the woods, and, as always, it really helped settle his nerves. Nothing like the warm sun, the soft sounds of nature, and the thrill of small discoveries to sweeten a sour mood. He spent some time on the shore of Winoka Lake—which was not much more than a big pond, really—sitting on his favorite smooth rock, just staring out over the gently rippling water and pondering the mysteries of the world. It was his number-one favorite place to be.

By the time he got back home to his lab, he was feeling reenergized and ready to get to work on his ancient discoveries. The fossils were interesting enough, but it was still that frozen oval thing that really fascinated him. He was surprised it was taking so long to thaw out, a whole day after he'd found it. He spent a good hour chipping off the ice and grit and hardened clay, one small chunk at a time, being extra careful not to scratch the perfectly smooth surface.

Certainly rocks with such a perfect shape didn't occur in nature. Or did they? Maybe it had been in a stream bed at one time, and the flowing water molded it into an oval. Actually, it looked more like a big petrified egg than a rock, but the only bird he knew of that laid eggs that size was an ostrich, and as far as he knew there were no ostriches in Wisconsin. Maybe there had been, thousands of years ago. Who knew? A trip to the library was definitely in order.

Once the object was quite a bit cleaner, Martin carefully lifted it up and placed it on a shelf next to his workbench, where he could stare at it and ponder it to his heart's content. To keep it from rolling off, he slid a few small stones from his collection underneath it, anchoring it in place. Then he unclipped a gooseneck lamp from the bench and attached it to the shelf, positioning it right over the stone. That way, he figured, not only would he be highlighting the showpiece of his rock collection (he liked his displays to have a dramatic flair, even though he was the only one who really ever saw them), but the heat from the lamp would also help melt off any leftover bits of ice.

As Martin stepped back to admire his sharp new display, into the barn walked his dad. This came as a big surprise to Martin, since (1) he was home very early, and (2) he hardly ever came out to the barn.

Martin knew something was up, and it wouldn't be good.

"Hey, sport," Mr. Tinker said cheerily.

"Hi." Martin felt like he'd been caught stealing a cookie or something. He tried to sound matter-of-fact. "You're home early."

"What do you mean? Six-thirty."

Martin checked his watch. It was actually almost seven. He'd completely lost track of the time.

He stood there, scratching his wrist, as his dad checked out his array of collected stuff.

"Sheez. What are you gonna do, open a museum out here or something?"

Martin forced a faint splutter, and just an instant later noticed a football in his dad's left hand. Yes, this was going to be trouble.

"Hey! Recognize this?" His dad held up the ball Mr. Fairfield had given them, grinning as though he were offering Martin a roll of hundred-dollar bills. "Let's try 'er out, eh?"

This let's-learn-a-sport thing was something his dad brought up every few months, usually with some new twist, but it never ended well.

Martin wore a vaguely lost expression. "No offense, Dad, but . . . I really don't think football is my forte."

"Your what?"

"You know. My strong point."

"How do you know if it's your forte if you never *apply* yourself to it? These things don't come easy, you know. You have to work at 'em."

Martin couldn't bring himself to say the obvious, which was that no amount of work was going to help. He was a natural klutz at every sport he'd ever tried, from bowling to thumb wrestling.

"The way I see it," his dad said, "you've got the best football genes of any kid in town, because you got 'em from yours truly. All you need to do is dig that natural talent out and polish it up a little bit."

"I think maybe I got Mom's football genes."

"Don't you believe it. Hey, football is not only a fun sport, but it's also a great character builder. And let me tell you something, kiddo. The football players get all the girls."

Martin's face was blank—he couldn't see the appeal in that at all. Mr. Tinker got the message and took a few steps back. "All right, here we go. Maybe I've been pushing you a little too far, too fast. We just need to start from the beginning, get the mechanics down. I'll coach you. Ready?"

"Shouldn't we go outside?"

"Nah, plenty of room. C'mon."

Martin reluctantly stepped away from his workbench, preparing for the worst.

"Okay, first thing. What you want to do is catch it with your hands, out in front of you. Like this. Not with your chest. Out. Okay? Here we go."

He made the softest of throws, and Martin—seeing only a cruise missile heading toward his face—instinctively turned his head away and threw his hands up in a panic. The ball thumped off his fore-arm and dropped to the floor.

"No, no, keep your eye on it," his dad said. "It's just a piece of rubber, it's not going to bite you."

Martin picked up the football and got ready to throw it back. But he felt like his pose was making him look more like a windup monkey than a quarterback.

"No, you're pushing it from your ear, like a girl. You want to bring it back, like this. Back. I told you that before, remember? Turn your body."

Martin's contortions made him feel even sillier. His dad stepped over and helpfully moved a few body parts around—a foot here, a knee there, an elbow someplace else altogether. When Martin almost looked like he might be able to deliver a real pass, Mr. Tinker returned to his spot and put up a nice target with his hands. "Okay. Let 'er fly."

Concentrating hard, Martin pursed his lips, took two little hitches, and whipped his arm forward with conviction. But the ball, apparently in no mood to be propelled through the air, simply slipped from his hand and plopped at his feet. Trying to minimize the embarrassment, he gave it a quick kick and it wobbled across the floor.

Looking like he'd just eaten a piece of bad cheese, his dad picked up the ornery pigskin. "All right, once more."

"Dad—"

"No, you've got to *believe* you can do it. It's all mental. Now remember, soft hands. Eye on the ball. *Guide* it in. Got it?" He tossed another powder-puff pass.

Determined to make the catch, Martin stepped forward and made a gallant grab for it. This time he did manage to get his hands on the ball—but in trying to get a grip on it, somehow he ended up launching it over his shoulder and straight onto his workbench, where it knocked over a bug display, scattered some tools, bounced straight up against the shelf, and banged directly on Martin's prize oval whatever-it-was. The thing tottered, came loose from its makeshift moorings—and rolled straight off the edge, heading for the floor.

Martin let out a gasp and instinctively leaped over—and made a perfect diving catch just before it hit the ground.

"Now, *that's* a catch!" his dad barked. "Why in the blazes can't you do that with a football?"

Martin wanted to answer, but all he could come up with was a strained smile and a shrug.

Mr. Tinker rubbed his brow as though stricken with a splitting headache. "We'll pick this up later. Maybe in the fall, eh? I'll take you to a Packers game or something. Go on in and get cleaned up for dinner."

As his dad marched out of the barn, Martin picked up a rag and gently wiped a few droplets of water— former ice chips—from the object's smooth surface; then he carefully returned it to its proper place on the shelf and centered it under the lamp. Any thoughts of football had already vanished from his head.

* * *

When class was over the next day, Martin managed to avoid Donald Grimes and headed straight for the public library. He'd been preoccupied with fossils and eggs and ostriches all day, and he was eager to do a bit of Internet searching and check out a few books.

His mom was on duty behind the desk, and she gave him a big smile as he walked in.

"Hi, squash blossom. How was school?"

"Fine. Mom, would you mind not calling me that?"

"Really?"

"It's kind of mooshy."

He could tell from her crinkled brow that this was a big disappointment to her. She had always called him mooshy names, but *really*. In *public*?

"Okay," she said, lips oddly twisted. Then she took a more businesslike tone. "Looking for something in particular today, sir?"

"Maybe a book about rocks. Or fossils. Geology stuff."

"Righto. That would be in section—"

"I know." Of course. He had checked out geology books before. "See ya."

As he headed off, she called after him, "Will you be needing a ride home, sir?"

"No thanks. I'm good."

Martin spent some time in the computer room, trawling the Net for whatever bits and pieces he could find about the many different kinds of fossils and how they form. But the sheer volume of information was a bit overwhelming, and it got kind of hard for him to sort out the good science from the bad. He always preferred to get his science info from books, anyway—it was generally more reliable, and he really liked having a solid thing in his hands that he could carry with him and delve into like a treasure chest of ideas.

So he headed into the stacks, made his way to the geology section, and started examining the book spines, looking for a title that might promise a few answers to the Mystery of the Oval Thing. *Gravel Pits of the Midwest*? Not likely. *Diamond Cutting and Valuation*? Nope, not that either. Ah: *A Book of Fossils*. Could be good.

The book was wedged in tight, and when Martin pulled on it . . . *kabloof!* The whole row of books tumbled off the shelf and scattered on the floor. "Great," he mumbled as he stooped down to pick them up. What really gave him a start, though, was what he saw through the gap on the shelf when he stood back up: the face of Audrey Blanchard, close up and in living color, her bright blue eyes staring at him through a sea of freckles, pencil tucked firmly behind her ear.

"It works better if you take 'em out one at a time," she said matter-of-factly.

In no mood for lame jokes, or for small talk with a stranger—well, an almost-stranger—Martin quickly picked up the rest of the books and slid them back onto the shelf. Audrey watched him coolly through the narrowing gap until he finally put the last book in place, blocking her completely. He didn't mean to be rude or anything; he was just caught off guard by her guest appearance. Besides, he was in the middle of something important.

Keeping the fossil book and a couple of others, he headed for the checkout desk.

Martin spent the rest of the afternoon in his lab, leafing through the library books and studying his fossils with a magnifying glass. He became more and more convinced that the hairy-looking thing was a big ancient spider, and he sifted carefully through the books in hopes of finding something to confirm his hunch. But the books turned out to be not much help; two of them had almost no pictures, and the other one was mainly about volcanoes and earthquakes. Those topics were certainly worthwhile, but they weren't likely to shed much light on the subjects of fossils and oddly shaped stones.

The volcano book turned out to be pretty interesting, though. Within the bright red covers were all kinds of colorful photos and drawings. Pretty soon it had him totally absorbed, and not thinking at all about his quarry discoveries.

After about ten minutes of reading, he heard a faint *bump* and looked over at the shelf to see that one of the stones anchoring the egg-shaped thing had slipped, and the big object had come loose. Martin carefully picked it up and looked it over. Somehow it felt lighter than before—he figured it was because the grit had been cleaned from it and the ice had melted. He certainly didn't want it rolling off the shelf again, so he grabbed a couple more stones and slid them underneath it.

Martin's dad usually came home late in the days before the Trout Palace opened for the season, but today he was reasonably early, so the Tinkers sat down for a nice, quiet dinner together. But when his parents got into a boring discussion about money, Martin didn't have anything to contribute; anyway, he kept thinking about how strange and scary it would be if a volcano suddenly blew open underneath Menominee Springs. Finally, he excused himself early and went back out to the barn.

He knocked out his homework in short order, then went back to the volcano book. He figured he would read for a while and then go back up to the house and watch a little TV before bed, but he got so caught up in all the stuff about vents and fissures and lava domes that before he knew it, it was ten o'clock.

He might have kept at it even longer if it weren't for something very odd that grabbed his attention: once again, a *thunk* came from the shelf.

The oval thing had shifted again.

What the . . . ?

He stood up and, eyes fixed on his prize object, warily stepped over for a closer look. He lifted it off the shelf and looked it over carefully. Why would it keep shifting out of place like that? It wasn't slippery. It wasn't lopsided. It wasn't especially heavy. He shook it, sniffed it, raised it to his ear. No answers to the mystery. Just coincidence, apparently.

He carefully placed it back on the shelf and grabbed a few more stones from his collection, pushing them underneath the oval thing on all sides. He checked and double-checked it to be absolutely certain there were no loose spots this time. When he was sure it was rock solid, he took a slow step backward.

Satisfied it would be okay now, he headed back to his chair to resume his reading. And the instant he sat down—*clunk!*

Martin let out a gasp and his gaze shot back over to the shelf. The egg thing had shifted again!

*What on earth is going on?* His muscles taut, his heart thumping, he took two tiny steps back over to the shelf and slowly reached for the object. He couldn't quite bring himself to touch it, as though he might get an electric shock. When his fingers were hovering just over the surface . . .

*Reep reep deedy bip!*

The sound made him nearly jump out of his skin. He knew instantly who was calling and why, but it was a minor distraction considering what was going on (or not) on that shelf. His eyes never left the oval stone as he picked up the phone and put it to his ear.

"Hi."

"What are you still doing down there?" Martin

could tell from his dad's sharp tone that he meant business.

"I'm just . . . um . . ."

"It's after ten. Get up here and get to bed."

"Okay . . . uh . . . five minutes?"

*"Now."*

"Please? I just have this—"

"I'm looking out the window, Martin. If I don't see your butt running across the yard in ten seconds, I'm gonna lock that barn up for good."

"Okay, but let me just—"

"One . . ."

"Wait, can I—"

"Two . . ."

"Okay. Coming."

Martin gathered his books and scooted out of there—though on the way, his eyes stayed fixed on that shelf as though drawn by magnetic force. He turned out the light only at the last possible instant before shutting the door.

Back at the house, he went through his usual bedtime routine, except tonight he was finished in half the usual time—teeth brushed, in his pj's, and ready for the sack in eight minutes flat. His mom, who was always at his bedside with a goodnight kiss, couldn't help but notice his speeded-up pace.

"You okay, pumpkin-puss?" she said as he buried himself under the covers.

"Sure."

"You seem a little . . . I don't know, twitchy?"

"I'm fine."

"Everything's okay at school?"

"Uh-huh."

She studied him, looking just a bit concerned. He squeezed out an innocent smile. It wasn't the most convincing smile he'd ever come up with, but it was enough to persuade her to let it go. "Okay. G'night, squash blos— G'night, sweetheart."

"'Night."

She gave him a kiss and left the room, turning off the light on her way out. *Finally,* he thought.

Martin listened closely for the sounds of his parents getting ready to turn in—the footsteps in the hall, the whispering voices, the water running in the bathroom. When he heard the *clunk* of their bedroom door closing, he jumped out of bed and scurried to the door to take a peek down the hall. Just a few seconds later, the sliver of light escaping from underneath their door blinked out.

Martin quickly slipped on his shoes, tiptoed down the stairs, and shot out the back door without even bothering to put on a jacket, even though the night was a bit chilly.

In no time at all he was back inside the barn, eyes fixed on that oval thing. It was right where it had been fifteen minutes before. He slowly walked over, reached up, and tapped it lightly with one finger, though he wasn't really sure what the point of that was. He leaned in close and put his ear right up next to it, and then, without stopping to think why, talked to it.

"Hello . . . hello . . . this is your captain speaking. . . . All ostriches report to the quarterdeck immediately—"

All of a sudden—the thing wobbled. Martin let out a gasp and jumped back, his eyes like saucers. It wobbled again.

"Holy mama," he half whispered.

It wobbled a third time, and this time it didn't stop. Martin swallowed hard and moved in a bit closer as it kept on rocking back and forth, twitching and shaking as though a volcano were about to blow up underneath it. Then . . .

*Crack!*

A jagged split shot across the surface. The object was shaking even harder than before. Brimming with excitement and curiosity, Martin reached up and took hold of the restless stone with both hands. He moved it slowly over to his workbench, where he could get a better look at the little drama unfolding in front of him. But before he could lay it there gently, there was another loud *crack!* He flinched and let go, dropping it on the tabletop—and splitting it completely open. The pieces of shell dropped away, and there it was, the eager being making its first appearance in the outside world . . .

A baby lizard.

*"Wow!"* Martin heard himself exclaim as the little creature slowly opened its eyes for the first time. It

flopped around on the table, trying to get some sort of foothold, then looked straight up at Martin, blinked once, and let out a raspy *squeak*.

*"Wow,"* he said again. As the newborn kept try-ing to get its footing, he couldn't help noticing that this was no ordinary-looking lizard. For one thing, it was bigger than any baby lizard he knew of—a good foot and a half long from head to tail. For another, its front legs were much smaller than its hind legs—too small to be useful for much of anything, it seemed. It was a grayish-brown color, and its head was too big for the rest of its body.

Obviously, the poor thing was deformed. In an odd way, Martin could relate.

The lizard finally managed to get itself into a somewhat upright position on its hind legs and gave a couple more *squeaks,* gazing at Martin with begging eyes. He wasn't quite sure what to do with that.

"Hello there."

*Squeak.*

"What do you want?"

*Squeak.*

"You want your mama, right?"

*Squeak.*

"I'm sorry, she's not here."

*Squeak.*

"No, really."

*Squeak squeak.*

Martin felt like he had to do something, but he wasn't sure what.

"Do you want me to—"

*Squeak squeak.*

"Okay. Okay. Hold on."

He reached down and slowly, gently scooped the lizard up in his hands. He brought it up close to his face, and right away it nibbled at his chin, like an affectionate puppy. Martin couldn't help giggling.

"I'm *not* your *mama,* you know."

A few weeks before, Mr. Eckhart had talked to the class about how a lot of baby animals bond to the first living thing they see; it's called imprinting. Martin wasn't sure he liked the idea of a lizard thinking he was its mother, but it looked like that was what he was going to get.

He locked gazes with the lizard, and the little thing just kept squeaking at him.

"What is it you want?"

*Squeak.*

"Are you hungry?"

*Squeak.*

"Yeah? What do you like to eat?"

*Squeak squeak.*

He looked around, then grabbed an empty cardboard box from the floor and put it on the workbench. "I'll go look for something. Wait here."

He lowered the lizard into the box, which the little thing did not appreciate one bit. It squeaked and thrashed around as Martin backed away.

"Just for a minute. I'm coming back. Really. Just wait."

He didn't know how long he could watch the creature's distress, so he forced himself to turn away and hurry out the door.

Martin sprinted across the yard to the house, not even thinking of what might happen if his parents caught him up and running around. He slipped through the back door into the darkened kitchen and made a beeline for the refrigerator. He swung the door open and stood in the bright light that flooded out into the room, scanning the bottles and jars and packages, hoping something would jump out and shout "Lizard food!"

But the food was not in a talkative mood, so Martin made his best guess and scooped up a loaf of bread, a head of lettuce, an apple, a jar of raspberry preserves, and a chunk of sharp Wisconsin cheddar. In grabbing the cheese from the back of the shelf, he managed to bang his elbow on a bracket, and before he could remember that he needed to keep it down, a loud noise escaped from his mouth.

*"Ouch!"*

It wouldn't have stung quite so much if he hadn't taken a direct hit on the cut he'd gotten when he fell through the rocks at the quarry. There was some fresh blood on there now, but Martin was less concerned about that than he was about getting caught by you-know-who. He held his breath, listening for the dreaded footsteps upstairs; but when they didn't come, he exhaled and quietly slipped back outside with his armload of lizard treats.

In the barn, he found the little lizard right where he had left it. Seeing Martin, it twitched and squeaked excitedly.

"See? I told you I'd come back." He dumped his stash of goodies on the table and peeled off a small piece of lettuce, holding it up over the box tantalizingly. "Look what I've got . . . nice and green. Lizards love leafy stuff, right?"

The lizard squeaked and did its best to take the lettuce, though its footing was still a work in progress. Martin lowered the leaf enough for the creature to grab it in its oversize mouth.

He watched as the little reptile chomped and chewed on the leaf—but it wouldn't swallow. Finally, it spat out the lettuce altogether and squeaked insistently at Martin.

"No greens, eh?"

*Squeak squeak!*

"Okay, then. I know what you want."

He picked up a knife from the shelf and cut a small piece of apple.

"Mmmm, apple. All sweet and delicious." He held the piece out, his own mouth opening wide in sympathy with the lizard's gaping jaws. The little beast yanked the apple out of Martin's hand and it fell to the bottom of the box, where the creature could get a good sniff before digging in. But after a couple of whiffs, it was clear that there would be no digging; the lizard turned away and went right back to its squeaking and squawking, seeming even more worked up than before.

"Really? You don't want fruit?"

*Squeak squeak squeak!*

"Okay. Well, this I know you'll like."

He opened up the bread package and tore off a tiny piece of crust.

"*Everybody* likes bread. Open the drawbridge . . ."

He reached into the box, and the lizard again stretched up and snatched the bread out of his hand greedily. But after three quick chomps, the verdict was the same: *ptui!*

As the scaly critter launched back into its screechy tantrum, Martin folded his arms on the edge of the box, lips taut, eyes squinting.

"You are a very picky lizard. Didn't anyone ever tell you beggars can't be choosers?"

The lizard suddenly lurched up and took a nibble of Martin's forearm. "There's not much else I can— Hey!" He had thought the licking and nibbling was just an affectionate nuzzle—until he realized that what it was nibbling on was the fresh blood on the scrape below his elbow.

Martin jerked away.

"What are you doing? You can't have that!"

The lizard twitched and squeaked. It wanted more.

At this moment, a little black spider, obviously not paying attention to where it was going, dropped down on its invisible silk strand and landed inside the cardboard box. The lizard spotted it right away, and with a ferocious look in its eye that would have been downright scary if it weren't just a baby, it lunged over and snapped up the unlucky bug, swallowing it in one gulp.

The lightbulb went on instantly in Martin's head.

"Ahhh, so *that's* what you want."

*Squeak squeeeeeeeak!*

"Okay, then. Don't move."

He grabbed his bug net and a jar and scurried outside. Light from inside the barn spilled out through a small window near the door, where a dozen or so white moths were fluttering around, looking for whatever it is moths look for when they fly into a light. Martin swooped his net, snagging a bunch of them in midair.

*Somebody* would be dining well tonight.

# FIVE

**M**artin could tell it was light when he woke up, but he didn't feel like opening his eyes; he was just too tired. Better to doze off again until the alarm went off. But even in his groggy state, something seemed off.

He felt a tickle on his cheek, and his hand jerked up to scratch it. Then there was a strange clicking sound in his ear, and it wouldn't stop. Knowing his night of sleep was over, he slowly opened his eyes—and what came into focus was a big reptilian face, just inches from his eyeball.

*Squeak.*

Martin leaped to his feet, partly from being startled and partly from now realizing he had fallen asleep on the barn floor.

"Oh, no. Oh, no," he muttered, trying to sort through

about a dozen thoughts at once. *What time is it? How could I fall asleep on the cold floor? Is anybody else up yet? Yikes, I'm in my pj's!*

The little lizard just looked up at him.

Martin's mind was a jumble, but one thing he realized was that time was not his friend just now.

"I've got to go."

*Squeak.*

"I know. Sorry, but I have to. Um . . ." He looked around, trying to focus his thoughts, and spotted a pile of old bricks against the far wall. He had an idea, and it was going to have to do for now.

Putting himself in high gear, he started bringing the bricks to the corner next to his workbench and building a little rectangular pen against the wall. The pen was about five feet square, and when he had built up the bricks to about a foot high, he scooped up the lizard and put it inside the enclosure.

The creature had been perfectly calm while watching Martin stack the bricks, but when it found itself trapped within the walls, it twitched and squealed like a monkey with its tail caught in a mousetrap.

"I know, but I can't stay! I have to go to school."

*Squeeeeeak!*

"Here . . ."

There were a few dead moths left over from last night's feast, and Martin dumped them into the pen.

"I'll get you more later, I promise."

*Squeak squeeeeeak!*

"Be patient, okay?"

He hustled toward the door, then made a quick U-turn, swept up the human-food leftovers from the workbench, and raced out.

When he got to the house, he could see through the window in the kitchen door that sneaking in would not be an option. His mom was rummaging in the fridge—no doubt looking for bread and jelly and apples—while his dad worked on a bowl of cereal at the table.

Martin tried to think of a plan. Maybe if he went around to the front door, he could slip in without being noticed . . . ? But wait. What about the food? Maybe he could just dump it in the woods.

His dad got up from the table and leaned out into the hall. Martin could hear him loud and clear as he called up the stairs.

*"Martin! Let's go, buddy!"*

He exchanged a few mumbled words with Mrs. Tinker, then hollered again.

*"Martin!"* He gave a shrill whistle, his patience clearly running out.

Deciding he'd be better off just to plunge in and hope for the best, Martin popped in the back door. His parents stared at him.

"Hi," he said, trying to be casual. "I, um . . . I went out early."

Dad seemed ready to deliver a few sharp words, but Mom spoke first. "You're going to be late. Go get dressed. Hurry."

Figuring the best way to end this conversation was

to get upstairs as fast as possible, Martin dumped his armload of food onto the table and scooted into the hall.

"Why did you take those?" Mrs. Tinker said.

"I had a sandwich," Martin called back as he raced up the stairs.

Before he escaped to his room, he heard his mom mutter, "A lettuce, cheese, and jelly sandwich?"

Mr. Tinker gave a muffled groan.

In class, Martin was so busy wondering and worrying about his new little friend that he could hardly pay attention at all. When Ms. Olerud called on him with a question about the Gettysburg Address, he blurted out "Stonewall Jackson," and the whole class cracked up.

"Martin," Ms. Olerud said. "You of all people, daydreaming. I'm shocked."

Normally he would have turned scarlet with embarrassment, but this time he didn't really care; he was too eager to get out of there and get home.

He wasn't entirely sure why he was so fascinated by that little deformed lizard. Maybe it was the way it had imprinted on him, and now he was feeling a bit . . . well, *motherly*. Or maybe he was also getting a bit of sneaky satisfaction from the whole thing, since he wasn't allowed to keep pets.

When Martin was six, he had begged his parents for

a hamster. When they finally got him one, he became very attached to the little guy, who he named Orville. One day, while he was playing with Orville in the yard, a hawk swooped down and carried him away, never to be seen again. Martin was so distraught that he barely spoke for a whole week. Finally, his parents had to take him to a therapist to help bring him out of his gloomy state. So after that they made a firm rule: no more pets.

Martin could kind of see their point. But that was a long time ago, and besides, he wasn't really thinking of the lizard as a *pet*. At least, not yet.


After class, Martin was in such a rush to get going that he forgot to scope out the schoolyard before leaving the building. Sure enough, when he got halfway across the yard, Donald and his two pals appeared right behind him.

"Hey, Tinkles, have you seen my shnorkus?" Donald said.

"Your what?"

"Maybe it's in here," Tyler said as he yanked off Martin's backpack.

"Yeah, let me see," said Donald, grabbing the pack. He dug into it and pulled the books out one by one, tossing them on the ground. "Hmm, that's not it. . . . Nope, not there . . ."

Martin gritted his teeth. "Grimes . . ."

"Wait, there? No . . ." Donald turned the pack upside down and emptied it out completely. "Guess not. Let me know if you see it, okay, Tinks?"

Donald and his friends strutted off, snickering and snorting. Martin stood there like he always did after Donald's torments, feeling like an idiot. At least it wasn't a wrestle, and he was grateful for that.

As he knelt down to gather his books, he was surprised when somebody picked one up and handed it to him. At first he thought Donald was back for round two, but when he looked to see who it was, he saw Audrey.

"Thanks," he mumbled. He had no clue what else to say, so he just finished picking up the books and dropped them in his pack. Audrey kept staring at him, calmly unwrapping a stick of gum and popping it into her mouth. Then she pulled another stick from the pack and held it up.

"Juicy Fruit?"

"No thanks."

"Guaranteed unchewed," she said as Martin hoisted the bag over his shoulder. He stood there for a moment, trying to think of something nice to say, but nothing came to mind in his present grumpy, embarrassed state. Besides, she was wearing a really bright green beret, and it distracted him. So, with a pitifully small and totally forced smile, he mumbled, "See ya," and headed for the gate.

Maybe he should have tried harder to be friendly, but he just couldn't understand why anybody would go out of their way to talk to him. What did she want? Anyway, he had urgent business to attend to and couldn't stop to chat.

Martin speed-walked to the library, where he found himself eighth in line to use a computer. Not wanting to wait, he headed into the stacks instead and checked out *A Field Guide to Reptiles*. His mom offered him another ride home, but he didn't want to wait for that, either, so he trotted back to the house on foot and, without bothering to stop off inside, went straight to the barn. And when he threw open the door, what he saw made his heart sink.

Tumbled bricks. Empty pen. No lizard.

"Oh, no!" he groaned as he stepped in to survey the situation. Why hadn't he been more careful building the wall? That lizard could be anywhere now!

Or could it? There was no way he knew for a creature that size to get out of the barn.

As he got set to start searching, he noticed something odd next to the workbench. He had put one of his bug-collection display cases on the floor when the lizard was on the tabletop the night before—and there was the case, right where he'd left it: empty! Every cricket, beetle, and butterfly in the case had disappeared, and the mounting pins were all bent, loose, or scattered around the floor.

"What the . . . ?"

Just as he picked up the display to assess the damage . . .

*Squeak!*

He turned around and saw his little friend, gazing up at him from the floor.

"You!"

*Squeak!*

"You are a very bad lizard. Bad! Those were *my* bugs."

*Squeak!*

"You have crossed the line, my friend. Just for that . . . just for that . . ." Martin tried to think of a fitting punishment, but nothing came to mind. The lizard was bobbing back and forth, obviously happy to see his "mom," and somehow punishment didn't seem like the way to go. "Okay, I'll let it slide this time. But don't let it happen again!"

He gently brought the lizard up to the tabletop, then opened the reptile book and took a deep breath, ready to get to work. But the critter made a lunge straight at another bug display, and Martin had to snatch it away.

"Hey! What did I just tell you?"

The lizard made a great big fuss, dancing and squeaking up a storm.

"Okay, I get it! Don't be such a brat."

He got up and grabbed his bug net. "I'll be back in ten minutes. Don't go anywhere."

He darted out of the barn and headed for the woods, but stopped short when he thought of something. *This guy has such a big appetite . . . I could spend the rest of my days chasing bugs. Maybe there's an easier way . . . ?*

He turned right around and ran up to the house,

where he retrieved a half-empty package of baloney from the fridge. His hunch turned out to be a good one: when he took the leftover lunch meat back to the barn, the lizard wasted no time digging in. It ripped and chomped and gobbled the stuff like a hungry hyena feeding on a zebra carcass.

Martin watched the whole thing with wide eyes. "Wow. You can really put it away, huh."

While the lizard worked on the baloney, Martin combed through the reptile book. There was some pretty interesting stuff in there, all right, but none of the lizards looked anything like this one. Mainly it was those deformed legs. The front ones were really tiny, and although the back ones were plenty big and strong, the feet looked like a bird's—three toes in front, one in back. There was one exotic lizard in the book that could run on its hind legs, but it didn't look at all like Martin's friend. Maybe being frozen in that egg for all that time had somehow mutated its genes, he thought.

As he leafed through the book, he kept talking to the lizard, as though somehow it might suddenly speak up and explain what was going on. "How come you don't look like any of these?" "Nah, you're way too big to be that one." "If you drop that baloney on the floor, I'm throwing it away."

But of course, he was talking to a reptile, and the reptile seemed perfectly happy to feast on the meat, wander around on the workbench, and completely ignore everything Martin said.

Still, Martin was thoroughly captivated by the little creature, and he couldn't help but smile as he watched it explore the tabletop like a curious kitten.

The blissful mood was instantly wrecked when his mom opened the door and stepped in.

"Martin, your room is a mess. You were supposed to pick it up."

Martin jumped to his feet, doing his best to block her view of the creature. "Oh, um . . . I forgot. Sorry."

"I need you to do it before dinner."

"Okay."

He was doing all kinds of twisty contortions to keep his frisky friend hidden, and his mom gave him an odd look. He smiled innocently, and that seemed to do the trick; she headed back out the door. But before she was gone . . .

*Squeak.*

The sound stopped her in her tracks, and she turned around to see the lizard trying to take a bite out of the reptile book.

"What in the world is *that*?"

"What?"

She gave him a withering look.

"Oh, this? It's, um . . . a lizard."

"I can see what it is. What's it doing in here?"

"I found him in the woods. His egg, I mean. He hatched."

"Martin, you know you're not supposed to bring wild animals in here."

"Actually, he's very tame."

"You know the rule: you can use the barn for your hobbies, but no pets, period."

The lizard was about to rip a page from a perfectly good library book, so Martin picked the little guy up, which it didn't seem to mind at all. But when his mom leaned in for a closer look, it *hissed* at her, backing her off.

"What's wrong with it? It looks deformed."

"He could be a mutant."

"Well, put it down, for gosh sakes. It could have all kinds of germs." She picked up the cardboard box from the floor. "Put it in here."

Martin didn't care for the direction this was taking, but he did what she said and gently put the lizard in the box. He felt a gray cloud descending over him as his mom let out a sigh and studied his face. Her voice was sympathetic but firm as she said exactly what he didn't want to hear.

"Honey, you'll have to let it go."

"Mom—"

"No, no buts. A rule is a rule."

"He can't survive out there alone. He depends on me."

"See? You're too attached to it already."

Martin felt he was older and wiser now, and could handle the emotional trials of having, or even losing, a pet. But he didn't sound very convincing as he made his case. "Really, I'm not. He's just a lizard. I know I can take care of him."

"Sweetheart, you can't keep an animal here.

Especially a sick one that you found in the woods. He'll have to go. Period."

Martin stood there silently. An empty feeling started just below his rib cage and spread all the way out to his fingers and toes.

"Right now. Roger that?"

He managed the tiniest of nods.

She gave him a little smile and ruffled his hair. "Fifteen minutes, then come up and do your room. I'm thinking there could be a nice surprise at dessert time."

She headed out, but stopped in the doorway with a puzzled look on her face. "There are lizards in *Wisconsin?*"

Martin gave a tiny nod; there were, though he wasn't too sure about this part of the state.

Still pondering it, she went out and headed back toward the house.

He looked down sadly at his beady-eyed little companion, dreading the next—and last—episode in their short acquaintance.

Martin carried the box a good distance into the woods, to a spot he never visited on his hikes. He knew the odds for the lizard weren't good out there, and he would just as soon not know how the story ended. A clean break would be best for all concerned.

He came upon a clearing with a small pond and decided it would be as good a place as any.

"How about here? You like this?"

The lizard just stared up at him from inside the box, as though wondering why they were in this strange place. Martin picked it up and put it down in a patch of tall grass.

"See? There's water . . . lots of bugs to eat . . . places you can hide. It's a good spot."

He expected it to skitter away like most animals do when they're set free. But it just stood there, calmly sniffing the ground. Martin made a shooing gesture, as though it were a pesky squirrel.

"Go on. Go."

The lizard still didn't move. Martin lunged at it, hoping to scare it off.

"Go!"

But the critter took only a single step back, without breaking its steady gaze at Martin's face.

"Okay, then. Don't go."

He turned and walked away. But what he was afraid of was exactly what happened: it followed him.

"No! Stay. *Stay.*"

He knew in the back of his mind that a reptile wasn't likely to understand a dog command, but he hoped for the best as he started off again. Again, the lizard followed.

Martin broke into a trot, thinking that maybe the little guy wouldn't bother trying to keep up.

He was wrong.

Deciding that strict measures were going to be called for, he scooped up the lizard, carried it to the other side of a big log that stretched across the forest floor, and put it down on the ground.

"You have to stay here! I'm sorry, but a rule is a rule. Good-*bye*."

He turned and marched away, knowing that was the last he would see of his little friend. Right away, a torrent of desperate squeaks and screeches came pouring out from behind that log.

The sound tore at Martin's heart, but he forced himself to keep going. *This is not like Orville,* he thought. *I'm older and wiser now. I am not attached to this lizard!* But the farther he got, the heavier his feet became. *It's just a dumb reptile. Let nature take its course!* He got a good fifty yards from the log, and he could still hear the lizard's squeals. They seemed to echo all around him, and he started feeling dizzy. He stopped to take a breath.

He was startled by a faint *whoosh* up above. What was that? A crow? A *hawk? Not already,* he thought. His palms were sweating, his heart racing. This was not right; it just wasn't.

Finally, he surrendered. *Leaving him out here would just be cruel,* he told himself as he headed back into the clearing, box in hand. He would have to deal with the consequences later.

By the time he arrived back at the barn, a good twenty minutes had gone by, so there was no time to waste.

But what to do with this animal that would now have to be kept a secret?

Martin had an idea.

At the other end of the barn from his work space, there was a trapdoor. It led down to a big storage room below the main level of the barn. There was a lot of old junk down there—wooden pallets, cardboard boxes, broken-down lawn equipment, a wheelbarrow, a rickety old bed frame—and it was on the dusty side. But some sunlight came in from a few small windows high on the wall, and since nobody ever went down there, it seemed like a workable home for a small creature without the brain power to imagine it could do better.

Martin opened the trapdoor and climbed down a steep wooden staircase, pushing away a few cobwebs as he reached the floor.

"You can stay down here," he said to the lizard, lifting it out of the box. "I'll bring you food and everything, but you have to be quiet. If anybody finds out you're here, we're both toast."

He held it up close to his face. "Do I make myself clear, young reptile?"

He knew the lizard had no idea what he was talking about, but it didn't complain.

"What's your name, anyway? You need a name." He thought about it, but not for too long. "Well, those beady eyes make you look kind of like my uncle Rufus. I guess that'll do."

He put the lizard on the floor, and it looked up at him with intense curiosity, like a toddler watching a puppet show.

"Well . . . see you later, Rufus."

Martin knew it would fuss and complain again the second he headed back up the stairs, and that was exactly what happened. This lizard did not appreciate being left alone.

After closing the trapdoor behind him, Martin knelt down and peeked into the room through a crack along the edge. He shifted around to keep the lizard in sight as it lurched back and forth, screeching up a storm. But after a few moments it seemed to forget what it had been carrying on about. It soon began exploring its new home a bit, and didn't seem to think it was so bad.

Then, it abruptly froze and crouched low.

With the quick reflexes of a cat, it darted after a cockroach that had skedaddled across the floor. And in the blink of an eye, the bug was on its way down the gullet of a lizard named Rufus.

# SIX

"**M**om," Martin said as she whipped up his favorite Saturday breakfast, apple-cinnamon pancakes. "Could I get my allowance?"

"That's your dad's department, love bug. You know that."

"Yeah, but he's at work."

"Are you in a rush?"

"Kind of."

She gave him a curious look but didn't start an interrogation. "Well, honey, I don't have any cash. Can you wait till he gets home?"

"That's okay. I'll ride my bike."

"Oh. To the Trout Palace?"

"Uh-huh."

And ride he did, his mind racing the whole way. If

Rufus was going to survive in that barn, he would have to be fed on a regular basis—and judging by his appetite, that could take some effort. Martin didn't want to have to be catching bugs all the time, and he was afraid if he kept filching food from the refrigerator, he would eventually get busted. So he was going to have to come up with his own food supply.

And that would require cash. Later on, he might be able to convince his parents that he was old enough to mow the yard for pay. But for now, he would have to rely on his usual source of income.

He made it to the Trout Palace in good time and found his dad in the Walleye Theater, driving two-inch screws into the stage floor. "You came here for *that*?" he said.

"I forgot to ask you yesterday."

His dad mumbled something that didn't sound quite like a real sentence, then put down his drill, reached into his pocket, and handed Martin a crisp Lincoln.

"Thanks!"

Mr. Tinker seemed like he might say something else, but within two seconds Martin was gone.

It took him less than five minutes to pedal to the Food Bear, where he headed straight for the meat department and spent two dollars and fifteen cents on a small package of raw ground beef. He didn't want to buy a lot at once, because he knew it wouldn't keep long and he didn't want to raise suspicions by storing it in the fridge. So there would probably have to be many trips to the market.

More and more thoughts like that came into Martin's head as he hopped on his bike and started for home. But all that thinking took his mind off his steering, and at the edge of the parking lot he ran into a curb and took a wicked header over the handlebars. Luckily he landed on a patch of soft grass and avoided any serious bodily damage. But the bike wasn't as lucky: the chain had been knocked clean off the gears.

"Oh, no," he grumbled as he checked it out, worrying more about the delay to Rufus's breakfast than the needed repair job.

"You okay, Martin?" The voice was familiar, but Martin was still a bit surprised to see his science teacher, Mr. Eckhart, approaching.

"Oh, hi. Yeah, I'm fine."

"Little mechanical malfunction there?"

"Can it be fixed?"

"Let's have a look."

As Mr. Eckhart put down his bag of groceries and got to work on the chain, Martin started thinking again. Maybe this would be a good time to clear up a few nagging questions.

"Mr. Eckhart, do you know a lot about animals?"

"Well, that's what they told me when they gave me my zoology degree. I guess I'll take their word for it."

"Zoology? I thought you were just, like, a general science person."

"Nah, I just teach you guys science to pay the bills while I work on my master's degree. Hope that doesn't disappoint you."

"No. . . . So . . . what kind of lizard has three toes—well, four, counting a little one in the back—and walks on two legs?"

"I give up. What kind?"

"No, it's a real question."

Mr. Eckhart looked at him with an arched eyebrow. "Okay, none of the above. Lizards have five toes and walk on four legs."

Martin spent a moment processing that. "So if a lizard has three toes and walks on two legs, that means he's a mutant?"

"Could be. Why?"

"Just wondering."

"Well, what you're describing sounds more like a bird than a lizard."

"Bird . . . ?"

"Yep. Or a dinosaur. There y'go. How's that?" He put the bike upright—chain back on, good as new. Martin hardly noticed.

"But dinosaurs are extinct."

"That is correct. Well, unless you count Barney."

He looked to Martin for a reaction, but he didn't get a chuckle, or even a smile. A thought was forming in Martin's head, and the joke didn't get through at all.

"Hello?" Mr. Eckhart said. "Unless you count *Barney.*"

Martin suddenly got a burst of energy. "Thanks!"

He jumped on the bike and raced off down the street, leaving his teacher standing there, his hands coated with grease, his face a picture of bewilderment.

All the way home, one outlandish thought rattled around in Martin's head. *A dinosaur?* The thought had occurred to him before, of course, but he had always dismissed it right off the bat. After all, there had been no dinosaurs for sixty-five million years. But then again . . . ?

When he got to the house he dropped his bike in the front yard and raced up to his bedroom. No need for a trip to the library this time; he remembered a book his mom had given him for his ninth birthday. It took only a short search to find it under some junk in the back of the closet: *All Things Dinosaur.*

In a flash he was off to the barn, stopping only long enough to throw open the fridge and grab a leftover Ultraburger from Royal Castle. He figured if Rufus was going to be chowing down on hamburger, well, then he would too.

He brought his reptilian friend up from his downstairs lair and lifted him onto the workbench. Even though he was only three days old, he already seemed heavier to Martin, and maybe an inch or two longer. "Don't eat it all at once," he said as he tore the plastic off the package of beef. "We have to make it last." As Martin expected he would, Rufus went right after the meat like a hungry puppy.

Digging into his own cold burger, Martin opened the dinosaur book and got down to business.

But it didn't take long for him to start thinking this whole project might not have been such a hot idea. The book had pictures and descriptions of all kinds of dinosaurs, but none of them looked at all like Rufus.

**HADROSAURUS.** Approximately nine feet in height, this dinosaur stood upright on its hind legs and had short forelimbs. Its most distinctive feature was its broad snout, shaped like a duck's bill . . .

Short forelimbs, okay. But there was no danger of anyone mistaking Rufus for a duck.

**CAMPTOSAURUS.** Camptosaurus had a thick body, and the juveniles often walked on two legs. With its sharp, toothless beak, it most likely fed on leaves, small branches, and tall grasses.

A beak? Leaves and grasses? Nope . . . nothing like *this* thing. Martin thought about it as he absently watched Rufus polish off the last of the raw hamburger.

Every time there was something in a picture or a caption that seemed like a match, there was something else that canceled it out. After twenty minutes of flipping through the book, Martin was starting to lose enthusiasm. "This is stupid," he grumbled. "Dinosaurs are *gone*. You're just a freaky lizard." He lifted the remaining half of his Ultraburger up to his mouth—and was startled when Rufus suddenly leaped up and chomped down on it, barely missing Martin's pinky.

"Hey!" he exclaimed as he watched Rufus twitch and tug, trying to tear off a piece of beef while hanging in midair by the grip of his tiny teeth. "That's mine!"

A corner of the bun gave way and Rufus dropped onto the tabletop with nothing to show for his sudden attack. But now he was all worked up, and he thrashed and squealed so annoyingly that Martin's resistance quickly wore down.

"Okay, okay! One piece."

He broke off a chunk of the burger meat and held it out toward Rufus, who snapped it away and dug right in.

"There's no *pigosaurus* in here. But I'm thinking that's you."

Martin let out a long breath and rubbed his eyes. Maybe later his dad would let him use his computer, and he could do a more thorough search.

Eyes glazing over, he idly leafed through the book again, stopping when he came to a page he vaguely remembered from his birthday two years earlier.

**TYRANNOSAURUS REX.**

He looked again at Rufus, who was tripping all over his own feet as he wrestled with his piece of the burger. Martin couldn't help but snicker.

"Right."

He held the book out next to Rufus, comparing him to the artist's drawing. Not much to go by, but might as well read on.

 **TYRANNOSAURUS REX.** T. rex was one of the most fearsome carnivores that ever lived. It was characterized by powerful hind legs with three forward toes and one back; tiny forelimbs with two toes . . .

He took a look at Rufus's shriveled forelimbs, which he hadn't really paid that much attention to before: two toes.

and long, sharp teeth. Though it was probably a scavenger of dead animals, it was most likely a powerful hunter as well, with a voracious appetite for meat.

As he watched Rufus tear away at the beef, Martin got an odd feeling. He held the book up next to Rufus again, and suddenly felt a strong tingling in the deepest caverns of his stomach.

"Noooo," he muttered, barely above a whisper. "It's crazy. It's ridiculous. No way!"

But his mind wouldn't let go of an alarming thought that just kept getting stronger and stronger. The next word that came out of his mouth surprised him and, even though he was the one who said it, actually scared him a bit.

"Way?"

Three eye-blinks later, Rufus finished off the last of the Ultraburger, looked up at his human companion, and emitted a sound that Martin could have sworn was a tiny reptilian belch.

# SEVEN

On the twenty-eighth of May, the Trout Palace opened for business.

Martin had talked his dad into getting him a job there, doing odd chores for pay. It wasn't a real *job,* of course—the child labor laws wouldn't allow it. But he knew his dad liked the idea of him getting out of that barn for a few hours a week and learning to fend for himself in the world. Martin really wanted to make a good impression on that first day, because then there was a good chance they'd let him work more hours when school let out for the summer.

Opening day was always busy, busy, busy, and Martin's assignment was just to wander the grounds and be available to help the visitors find their way around. This was not his favorite thing to do (talking with strangers—ugh!), but he put on his best face and mingled in with the crowd in his too-big Trout Palace Staff T-shirt, with a big red-and-yellow HOW CAN I HELP YOU? button pinned prominently on his chest.

The Trout Palace was nothing new to Martin, but even he couldn't help feeling a bit of excitement as the guests eagerly streamed into the park by the hundreds.

In the outdoor area, the Ferris wheel, the merry-go-round, the "Rocket" mini coaster, and all the other rides sprang to life, calling out to the youngest fun seekers like a living toy box. It was a warm, perfect spring day, and the shimmering colors and cheery music blended with the kids' delighted screams to lend a real sense of excitement to the occasion.

As people came in the front entrance of the main building, the first thing they saw was the giant fish hanging from the ceiling. Just as it had every day for years, it greeted the visitors in a loud, deep voice, its lower jaw bouncing up and down like a marionette's:

*Ho ho ho ho! Welcome to the Trout Palace!*
*Thirty acres of pure Wisconsin fun.*
*If you like it, we've got it—*
*so come on in, leave your worries outside,*
*and get set for the time of your life!*
*Ho-o-o-o-o-o ho ho ho ho!*

By the end of the day, Martin and the other workers would be so sick of hearing that talking trout that they would dream of smashing it to pieces with a heavy stick, like a giant piñata. But the visitors seemed to like it just fine.

Once they were inside, the guests could head in almost any direction and find something fun to do. Straight ahead was the long midway, a busy boulevard of carnival attractions—mainly food stalls and all kinds of games of skill and chance, including, naturally, that goofy U-Bag-Em game. At the far end of the midway, a huge room full of arcade games kept dozens of kids—mostly the older boys—occupied for hours at a time.

Just to the left of the main entrance was the Heart o' the Woods restaurant, where you really could catch your own dinner. A set of large doors led from the dining room to an outside patio, and the patio jutted out over a big, man-made pond. The pond was kept well stocked with rainbow trout and lake perch—easy game for adventurous diners with fishing poles supplied by the restaurant. Master chef Tim McTavish would then clean, cook, and garnish their catch for a delicious dinner.

A few yards beyond the restaurant entrance was where the "Four Muskrateers," Daisy, Edna, Walter, and Fritz, delighted all comers by racing down a long, winding wooden track. All they were really interested in were the muskrat treats at the finish line, but the human spectators, who could make bets on the outcome of the race with play money, found the whole thing perfectly charming.

And if muskrats weren't your cup of tea, well, there were always Zippy and Flippy, the furry stars of the always-popular "Ballet de Beavre." How they taught those big rodents to dance and prance around that little stage wearing fluffy white tutus, and to do it a dozen times every day, is a mystery only a beaver's brain can fathom. But their rendition of *Swan Lake* never failed to entertain and inspire.

Another audience favorite, especially with the kids, took place in the Walleye Theater. The stage was home to magicians, acrobats, jugglers, and novelty acts of all descriptions. The show's masters of ceremonies were "Curtis and Jake," a pair of backwoods dimwits who kept 'em laughing with a nonstop barrage of bad puns, slapstick routines, and big, toothless grins. Many of the folks in Menominee Springs didn't much appreciate being portrayed to the world as dumb country hicks, but as long as visitors kept buying tickets to the shows, Ben Fairfield didn't concern himself with such things.

By the end of the day, Martin's feet felt like they had sandbags attached to them, and he leaned against a railing to give them a bit of a break. He could see Mr. Fairfield standing in his usual spot just below the talking fish, greeting the arriving customers with a handshake and a smile. "Hi there, folks! Thanks for coming today."

He seemed happy enough, but in between groups

of guests his expression darkened, and he fidgeted tensely. Martin had sensed his mood all day and kept his distance, but his dad wasn't afraid to walk up to him. "Little slow for opening day, eh, Ben?"

"Disaster," Mr. Fairfield snapped. "Worst in twenty years."

"I wouldn't sweat it based on one day. Whole season to go yet."

The words of encouragement didn't help, and Mr. Fairfield marched away gruffly.


For Martin, this job meant some extra dollars in his pocket for spending cash. And as the owner of a rapidly growing pet with a giant appetite, he needed a *lot* of spending cash. He was amazed at how fast Rufus had grown in just five weeks—and how much food he put away. At first, Martin collected as many dinner scraps and leftovers as he could take without raising suspicions, but pretty soon it just wasn't enough. So he had to do the one thing he had sworn he never would: he raided the mayonnaise jar holding his life savings—all forty-eight dollars and twenty-six cents of it. He used every penny to buy dozens of cans of a dog food called Fido-Nummy, because it was cheap and Rufus liked it.

And the bigger Rufus got, the more Fido-Nummy he ate. Martin was keeping a log of his growth, and he could hardly believe how fast the numbers went up:

| WEEK | LENGTH (nose to tail) | HEIGHT | GIRTH (belly) | WEIGHT (approx.) |
|---|---|---|---|---|
| Week 1 | 1 ft. 10 in. | 1 ft. 1 in. | 7 in. | 8 lb. |
| Week 2 | 2 ft. 5 in | 1 ft. 7 in. | 11 in. | 23 lb. |
| Week 3 | 3 ft. 1 in | 2 ft. 3 in. | 15 in. | 37 lb. |
| Week 4 | 3 ft. 9 in. | 3 ft. 0 in. | 19 in. | 52 lb. |
| Week 5 | 4 ft. 7 in. | 3 ft. 7 in. | 23 in. | 66 lb. |

The weight measurements weren't quite exact, because Martin had a hard time holding Rufus on his mom's bathroom scale, which he would occasionally borrow while she was at work. But he figured his numbers were pretty close.

By the time the Trout Palace had been open for a week, Martin's money supply was about gone, and the Fido-Nummy was dwindling fast. He had put in a good ten hours of work there, and he needed to get paid, and soon. At the end of that warm Friday, he spotted his dad replacing a lightbulb on the U-Bag-Em and briskly walked up to him.

"Hi, Dad. I finished washing those tools."

"Huh? . . . Oh. Yeah."

"So . . . is that it?"

"Um . . . did you sweep up the theater like I said?"

"Uh-huh."

"Sanded the splinters off the thing . . . ?"

"Yep."

Martin stood there, nervously scratching his shoulder, as Mr. Tinker kept wrestling with the hard-to-reach bulb, grunting under his breath.

"Okay," Martin finally said. "Guess that's it." He trotted off toward Ben Fairfield's office.

"Where're you going?"

"Mr. Fairfield said I'd get paid on Fridays."

"No, don't bother him. I'll get it from him later. Here." He took out his wallet and extracted a few bills. But he didn't hand them to Martin right away; instead he just stood there, studying him.

Martin figured he was about to get a lecture or something, and he was not incorrect.

"Y'know, Marty . . . maybe you're right. Maybe football isn't your forty-ay."

"Forte."

"Not everybody can be Aaron Rodgers. Now, *hunting* . . ." He took hold of the mounted rifle and aimed it into the fake woods. "*There's* a sport where you don't have to be big, or even that coordinated. Maybe I'll take you up to Collin Cove next fall. Bag yourself a duck or two."

"Okay. Could you please pay me now? I'm in kind of a hurry."

Martin could tell from his dad's narrow squint that he was hoping for a better answer than that. Luckily, though, he didn't press the issue, and grudgingly handed the bills to Martin.

"Don't spend it all on bug nets."

"I won't. Bye."

Martin knew his parents' expectation that the Trout Palace job would get him out of the barn and into the world didn't work out as they had hoped. One night he overheard them talking about how he seemed even more withdrawn than before, and was spending even more time by himself in the barn. It worried them.

But of course, he was not by himself. Being with his rapidly growing dinosaur quickly became the thing Martin cared most about in life. Unlike the humans he knew (except his mom), Rufus was always excited to see him when he got home from school or work. And he seemed to thrive down in that big cellar, always gobbling down the scavenged scraps and Fido-Nummy that Martin brought. Martin didn't even mind shoveling up the increasingly large piles of dino poop and hauling them out to the woods.

In the back of his head, he knew there was a chance that this could turn into another Orville-the-hamster situation. But as Rufus grew, it seemed pretty obvious that no hawk would be foolish enough to come after him. Not only was he getting too big for that, but his teeth were becoming quite prominent, and his reflexes were as quick as a cheetah's. And Martin didn't want to risk taking him out of the barn anyway—not only might Rufus get discovered, but he might like it too much. Either way, Martin didn't spend a lot of time worrying that he might be getting too attached to his secret pet.

Ms. Olerud spoke the words aloud as she wrote them on the board.

"Although today is the last day of school . . . we have to finish our English lesson."

She turned to the class. Everybody already had their minds on summer vacation, so feet were shuffling, eyes were wandering, and lips were whispering. Even Martin had to concentrate to keep from fidgeting.

"Okay, settle down, now, settle. This is what kind of sentence? . . . Brianna?"

"Complex," Brianna Hogan replied.

"Very good," said Ms. Olerud as she turned and wrote "complex" on the board.

It was a good thing she didn't call on Donald Grimes, because he wasn't paying attention at all. He was idly spinning a thumbtack around on his desktop, mouth hanging open, no doubt daydreaming about all the fun he was going to have starting in less than an hour.

His seat was right behind Audrey Blanchard's, and as he stared into her back, suddenly his eyes opened wide and his forehead crinkled up. Martin caught a glimpse of his face, and knew all too well from experience that that expression meant trouble. After throwing a devilish grin across the aisle to his buddy Nate, Donald slowly leaned forward and ever so carefully pushed the thumbtack through the hem of Audrey's yellow linen skirt and deep into the wood of her chair.

Donald and Nate could barely keep from cracking up at what they hoped and expected would come next. And they didn't have to wait long, because it was only a few seconds later when Ms. Olerud turned back to the class.

"Okay, who thinks they can diagram it?"

Audrey's hand sprang up, as usual.

"Audrey. Give it a shot."

Audrey's fate was sealed. As she got up and headed for the board, the sound reverberated throughout the classroom: *rrrriiiiippppp!!!*

The whole class broke out in a roar of laughter as Audrey looked down at her badly tattered skirt. Grimacing, she quickly grabbed the torn pieces of fabric and pushed them back together, twisting herself into a pretzel to try to preserve some shred of modesty.

"All right, that's enough!" Ms. Olerud barked. *"Quiet!"*

But it was too late. The laugh fest had taken on a life of its own.

Ms. Olerud didn't catch on to Donald's treachery. "Come on, honey," she said as she led Audrey, face as red as her hair and lips all twisted, toward the door. "You kids are being very mean!"

Audrey took one sidelong glance at the roomful of laughing faces, all bug-eyed and stretched out like grotesque circus clowns, as she and Ms. Olerud went out. There was only one person who knew what Audrey must have felt like, and he wasn't laughing at all. That was Martin Tinker.

The final bell rang, and kids exploded out of the building in a big, noisy, joyous blob. Summer at last!

Not one for such mindless displays of emotion, Martin walked out calmly amid the jubilant crowd, his now-empty backpack in his hand, trying his best to dodge all the flying knees and elbows. But he had barely reached the bottom of the steps when he heard a familiar voice right behind him.

"Get rid of this, Tinkleberry! It's summer!"

With one lightning-quick move, Donald Grimes snatched away Martin's backpack and heaved it up in the air—where the strap caught neatly on a branch of a big elm tree hanging over the fence into the schoolyard. Delighted with his perfect aim, Donald let out a shrill "Wooo-hoooo!" and lumbered on his way.

Except for the occasional butt pinch or ear flick, Donald hadn't hassled Martin all that much for the past few weeks. And Martin had figured he wouldn't bother with it on a happy day like this one, so he had let his guard down. Oh, well.

With a sigh, he trudged over and looked up at his tree-borne backpack. He tried jumping up to grab it, but it was just out of reach. So he jumped again . . . still not quite. He made a few more jumps, feeling like an idiot—and drawing laughs from some of the nearby kids—but never quite getting his hand on it.

Suddenly, a short, heavy stick flew up and thwacked on the backpack. It came loose from the branch and plopped at his feet. He looked to his left, and there stood Audrey Blanchard—her skirt neatly reassembled with safety pins, her freckled face carrying a strange, unreadable expression.

"Thanks," Martin muttered self-consciously as he picked up his bag and headed out the gate. He figured that would be the end of that, but he was a bit startled to notice she was walking right next to him—and even more startled when she spoke.

"How come you didn't laugh?"

"Huh?"

"You were the only one."

"Wasn't that funny."

They walked on in silence. Martin could feel the sweat building up in his pores. He and Audrey hadn't exchanged more than a dozen words since the day she arrived—the last time they'd spoken at all was when he ran off after she helped with his fallen books. Why was she talking to him now? Hoping to end it, he quickly cut across the street. But five seconds later, there she was again, walking right behind him. He walked faster. So did she. He tried to ignore her, but when he got a strange sensation and glanced back, there she was, doing a comical imitation of his mopey walk. She gave him an impish smile, but all he could do was roll his eyes.

With a dramatic sigh, she put it straight to him.

"Martin, what is the deal with you?"

"What do you mean?"

"I don't get you. You're the only one who's ever sort of, like, almost nice to me, but then you won't even talk to me."

"I'm talking to you now."

"This is not talking. This is me throwing out words and you slapping them away like bugs. I mean, *geez*. You act like you don't even *want* any friends."

"Nobody wants to be friends with me."

"How do you know?"

"They all think I'm weird."

"Really? They call *me* Tippi Tomato. How do you think *that* feels?"

"I dunno."

"But at least I'm trying. With you it's like, you just *gave up* or something. I mean, you do *want* friends, don't you?"

Martin's brain seized up. She was touching a nerve here.

"Okay," she said, "I'll start. Hi, Martin. Wanna do something?"

Actually, what he had been hoping to do, since he didn't have to work today, was go home and spend some time with his nonspeaking friend. But he wasn't thinking straight in the stress of the moment, and he couldn't figure out how to say no.

# EIGHT

They decided to go hang out at Martin's house for a while, since it had been a short school day and his mom wouldn't be home for at least a few hours. It was a fifteen-minute walk to get there, and to his surprise and relief, talking to her was easier than he expected. Actually, Audrey did most of the talking, and by the time they got there he knew more about her than he figured he would ever need. Her dad was a lineman for the power company; her mom died when she was three; her middle name was Alicia; she was allergic to cows; her favorite color was purple; she could sing "Yellow Submarine" in three languages.

When they got to Martin's house, they headed straight for the kitchen, sat down at the table, and started fixing themselves a couple of peanut butter and jelly sandwiches.

"Jade never lets me eat stuff like this," Audrey declared. Jade, she had told him on the way over, was her seventeen-year-old sister, an eleventh grader at Menominee Springs High.

"Why?"

"She says it's junky. I think it's okay, though. I mean, nuts, fruit . . . healthy, right?"

"I guess so."

There was a brief silence as they both spread the strawberry jam across the bread.

"So what's the deal with the pencil?" he asked.

"What about it?"

"It's always there."

She shrugged. "You never know when you might need to jot something down." Her eyebrows went up. "Speaking of which . . ."

She pulled a little notepad out of her skirt pocket, touched the pencil tip to her tongue, and started scribbling.

He leaned over to try to get a peek, but she pulled it back. He tried leaning in farther, and she pulled back even more. She smiled, and they both giggled.

"Quick, what's this?" She pocketed the pad, stuck her fingers in the sides of her mouth, and twisted her face into a jack-o'-lantern.

"What."

"Donald Grimes on a *really* good day."

They both had a good laugh at that one. Martin realized he wasn't feeling quite so tense anymore.

"So what do you wanna do?" she asked.

"Well . . . we could watch *The Simpsons.*"

"Mm, nah . . . that's boring. Anyway, Jade says too much TV rots your brain."

"Jade is like your mom, huh?"

"Yeah . . . my dad's always working, so she takes care of me. Stinky job, but somebody's gotta do it, right?"

They both smiled, and then went quiet again. Not one to let a silence stand, Audrey spoke.

"So what do you do when you're not at school?"

"Hmm, well . . . some days I work at the Trout Palace."

"Yeah? I've never been there. Is it fun?"

"It's okay," he said with a tiny shrug. "What about you?"

"Well, let's see . . . I like to read, and I like to write. I'm working on my first great novel."

Martin nodded. Now the pencil made sense. He was about to ask her what her novel was about, but she spoke up first.

"Your turn. What else?"

"What else what?"

"What else do you *do,* dummy?"

"Oh, you know . . . this and that."

"Like?"

"Just . . . whatever."

"Martin . . ."

"I collect stuff."

"What kind?"

"Rocks . . . bugs . . . leaves."

"Can I see?"

"Mm . . . not that much to see, really."

"You're being modest, right?"

"No."

"I want to see. Let me see."

Martin wasn't so sure he wanted anybody else in that barn. It was his private space.

On the other hand, he *was* proud of his collections, so why not show them off for a change? And as for Rufus . . . well, he was safely locked away on the lower level, so there was no reason to worry that the big secret would get out.

So off they went to the barn.

As Martin showed her his collections, he found himself doing a lot of talking—well, for him, anyway. He was kind of surprised that Audrey actually seemed interested, even when he called things by their scientific names. She loved the butterflies, especially the tiger swallowtail and the red admiral. And when he opened up the rock collection, she immediately gave a little gasp and picked one of them up, a beautiful, sparkling crystal.

"What's this one?"

"Amethyst."

"Wow! I love purple," she reminded him.

"You can have it."

"Really? No."

"It's okay. I've got another one."

"Wow. Thanks, Martin!" She scanned over the other stones in their mounting boxes. "This stuff is so cool. Where did you get it?"

"Out in the woods."

"You go in the woods?"

He nodded.

"My dad would never let me do that. He thinks the woods are full of, like, mad killers and whatever. What's this?" She picked up Rufus's growth chart, which Martin had completely forgotten was sitting on the table in plain sight. He snatched it away and put it facedown on the shelf.

"Oh, that's nothing. Just . . . one of my . . . projects."

He just knew she would start asking questions, but another thought grabbed her.

"Oh! I should probably call Jade."

"Okay."

"I don't have my own phone. Can I use your—"

*Yerp!*

The sound was kind of like a chirp from a big bird, or maybe a bark from a small dog.

"What's *that*?"

"Hm?"

He knew exactly what it was, but he was almost as surprised by it as she was. Rufus had never made a sound like that before. And when he did make noises, it was only when Martin went down there. Rufus must have heard the voices, and was wondering where his supper was.

*Yerp!*

"There!" said Audrey. *"That."*

"I didn't hear anything. Know what, I left my phone in the house. Let's just—"

He tried to hustle her out of there, but Rufus was not cooperating.

*YERP!*

"Martin! There's an animal in here."

"Oh, that? No, that's just . . . um . . ." Martin desperately needed a good lie. But his mind went totally blank. So he said the only words that came into his head. "That's my, um . . . lizard."

"You have a lizard? Can I see him?"

"Ohhhh . . . nah, you don't wanna—"

"Yes, I do. I love animals. Come on, Martin. Let me see your lizard."

Martin realized that his big secret was about to be a secret no more. But he also knew, in the back of his mind, that maybe he kind of wanted it to happen this way. He really needed somebody he could trust, and even though he wasn't totally sure that Audrey was the one, she was the only candidate just now.

He led her to the other end of the barn and unloaded a few bricks from the top of a pile. Underneath was a stack of unopened cans of Fido-Nummy.

"You can see him," he said as he lifted out one of the cans, "but you can't say one word to anybody, okay?"

"Why not?"

"I'm not supposed to have a pet."

"You feed your lizard *dog food*?"

"He's not your usual lizard."

They stepped over to the trapdoor and Martin lifted it open.

"You don't have to be afraid of him. He's big and he looks kind of mean, but he's not dangerous or anything."

"Martin, I'm not some delicate petunia. I'm not afraid of an old lizard."

He climbed down the creaky wooden steps, and she followed. They reached the floor and stood facing each other, the shafts of afternoon sunlight streaming in through the high, recessed windows. For a few seconds, it was very quiet.

"So? Where's the cage?" she said.

"He's not in a cage."

"Okay, so . . . let's see him."

"Don't turn around real fast."

"Ha ha, funny. Come on, just show—"

A puff of moist air washed over the back of her neck, and she froze.

Rufus was right behind her, sniffing out this odd new creature in his lair. Standing on his sturdy hind legs, he was now a good four feet tall—not much shorter than they were—and with his full array of claws and sharp teeth, there was no mistaking what kind of beast he was.

So when Audrey slowly turned around and found

herself face to face with a wide set of razorlike chop-pers and a pair of red reptilian eyes, she did what any normal girl would do: she let out a piercing *scream* that could wake the dead.

Rufus gave a loud *hiss* and bolted in the other di-rection, trying to climb a pile of junk but just stum-bling around clumsily. Audrey, meanwhile, darted behind Martin.

"Get it away get it away get it away!"

"Shhhh! You have to be quiet!" He went over to try to calm his jumpy dino.

"Martin, what *is* that?!"

"My lizard, I told you."

"You call *that* a lizard?"

"A dinosaur, actually."

"A *what?*"

Rufus seemed in a near panic, desperately trying to climb a wall to escape this noisy human. Martin gently put his arms around him.

"Rufus, relax. She's not going to hurt you."

"A *dinosaur?*"

"Come on, boy, you have to meet her. She's not so bad."

"Oh, thanks. Ai-yai-*yai* . . ."

Rufus calmed down a bit, and Martin managed to pull him toward Audrey—who let out an unsteady "Gahhh" and backed away.

"Stay there," Martin said. "He needs to know you're not afraid."

"Who says I'm not?"

"You did." He kept edging Rufus toward her. "Come on, boy. She won't bite you. I promise."

"*I* won't bite *him*?"

"See? . . . She's just a girl."

He got Rufus just close enough to Audrey so he could stretch out and give her another good sniff. She stood there like a toy soldier at attention and emitted the tiniest of squeaks.

"You can pet him." He gently ran his hand across the back of Rufus's head. "Try it."

"I'm not touching that thing."

"It's okay. He likes it. And he *really* likes *this*."

He scratched Rufus under the chin, and the big creature tilted his head back and squinted his eyes like a contented basset hound.

Audrey looked like she was watching somebody eat a worm. "You know what, Martin? You *are* weird."

"Go ahead."

She swallowed hard and very slowly reached her hand toward Rufus. But before she could touch him, he gave a sharp *hiss* and snapped his teeth, backing her off in a hurry.

Martin gave him a little smack on the snout. "No! *Bad* T. rex. We don't bite people. Roger that?"

"Did you just say *T. rex*?"

Rufus seemed a bit calmer now, so Martin gently pushed him toward her again.

"Okay. Try it."

"Pass!"

"He'll be okay now. I promise."

She exhaled deeply, rolled her eyes, and slowly reached for Rufus's head one more time. Rufus kept an eye on her, but he didn't complain this time as she touched the tips of her fingers to the back of his neck and stiffly stroked up and down, a lemon-puckered look on her face.

"See?" Martin said. "He likes it."

"I don't believe this. I'm petting a vicious prehistoric beast."

"He's not vicious."

"Martin, this is majorly crazy. Dinosaurs are extinct."

"That's what *I* thought."

She gasped and jerked back as Rufus suddenly broke away and went after the can Martin had put on the ground.

"Slow down, Rufus," he said as he pulled the top off the can and got set to whip up a good dino lunch.

It didn't take long for Rufus to polish off his meal, or for Audrey to start feeling a bit more comfortable around him. Martin told her all about the quarry and the egg, and how Rufus had imprinted on him as soon as he hatched. Rufus seemed to get more comfortable with Audrey, too, and before long they were like three old friends, just hanging out on an early June afternoon.

Martin was glad he had let Audrey in on his secret;

she seemed like somebody he could talk to, and he felt confident she wouldn't blab.

"Do you ever take him outside?" she asked.

"Not really."

"He'd probably run away, huh."

"I don't think he would. He's really attached to me."

"Or somebody might see."

Martin shrugged.

"You'll have to take him out sooner or later, though, right?"

Martin thought about it, and he realized she was absolutely right. "Okay," he said, heading for the stairs. "Let's take him out."

"What, *now*?"

"Sure. Why not?"

"Well . . . I don't know, I was just kind of like . . . throwing it out there."

"We'll just go for a few minutes."

"What if he runs away?"

"He won't."

"But you don't know for sure."

Martin really wasn't too worried about it, but to put her mind at ease he found a length of old clothesline and knotted it into a leash, then gently dropped the loop over Rufus's head. Rufus twitched and thrashed at first, not at all happy having a rope tied around his neck; but after a couple of minutes he seemed to forget it was there.

There was a pair of creaky old wooden doors that

led from the barn's lower level straight out into the far end of the yard. But they hadn't been opened in ages, so Martin had to go outside and pull away a bunch of weeds and brush that were blocking them. He finally managed to get one of the doors partway open, and Audrey poked her head out.

"Know what I forgot?"

"What."

"I have to call Jade."

"We'll just be a few minutes. Can you call her when we get back? It's only three o'clock."

She seemed a little unsure. "Okay."

"Ready?"

She nodded and handed the end of the leash to him, and they both pushed the door the rest of the way open.

At first, Rufus hesitated to step out into this odd, unfamiliar world. Martin thought maybe he remembered that scary day when he was almost left all alone out there. He finally stepped through the door, looking around, taking a few sniffs of the grass at his feet.

"Well," Audrey said, "I guess he— *Whoa!*"

She had barely gotten the words out when Rufus, spotting a sparrow as it rocketed through the air from the yard into the woods, made a sudden dash after it.

The leash immediately went taut in Martin's hands, and he was yanked right along with the charging dinosaur. "Hold on, Rufus!"

"Ai-yai-yai!" Audrey cried, and she quickly grabbed the leash to help Martin hold on.

Between the two of them, they were able to halt Rufus's mad dash. But he was over eighty pounds of pure muscle now, and he kept tugging and twisting, trying to get free of the rope. Martin and Audrey held on for dear life.

"You said he wouldn't run!" she hollered.

"I might have been wrong on that."

"Oh, great."

Rufus somehow managed to get the rope between his teeth, and in a flash—*snap!* All they held now was a loose piece of rope, and Rufus was hurtling into the woods after the little brown bird, his powerful hind legs pumping like a Thoroughbred's.

"Ohhhhh!" Audrey rasped. "Not good. Not good!"

"Rufus! Come back here!"

They raced into the woods after him. By now the sparrow was long gone, but Rufus was so excited by all the other birds flapping around in the brush that he dashed every which way, trying to snap one up in his hungry jaws. The birds were much too fast, though, so his only meal was a big helping of fresh Wisconsin air.

He spotted a chipmunk hopping along a log; again, instinct took over and he lunged after it—until it easily escaped up a tree.

A butterfly flitted past, and he snapped at it twice, three times, four times, trying to turn it into a light snack. But it was just too quick.

Rufus wasn't having much luck catching anything, but he did succeed in causing a near panic among all the small animals within fifty yards. A rabbit dashed into the underbrush, squirrels shot up into the trees, frogs leaped into a pond, and in the sky overhead a flock of restless crows sounded a shrill alarm.

Martin and Audrey tried their best to keep pace with their charged-up friend, but he was amazingly nimble, springing in and out of the brush like a spry fox, and they fell way behind.

"Rufus!" Martin shouted. "You come back here this instant!" For some reason he decided that the stern-parent approach was the way to go, even though his logical mind understood that this human concept would most likely be lost on a six-week-old prehistoric brain.

Before they knew it, Rufus was completely out of sight.

"Ohhh, man," Audrey moaned. "Ohhh, man. Now what are we—"

"Shhhh!"

Martin went perfectly still and listened. Audrey did the same. Their eyes slowly scanned the trees and brush on either side of the path.

A faint hissing sound, kind of like a leaky steam pipe, seemed to be coming from a small thicket across the way. As they tried to zero in on the spot, the hiss suddenly got much louder, and then it turned into a full-out *yowr!* Rufus jumped straight up in the air as a snarling snout with bared teeth and a set of cutlass-like claws lashed out at him.

Rufus leaped out of the thicket and hightailed it

through the brush and brambles, straight back to his own human "mom."

"Rufus!" Martin exclaimed, half laughing, as Rufus darted around behind him, cowering like a frightened puppy. "You bad boy! What did you do?"

"What *was* that?" Audrey said.

"There's a badger burrow over there. He must have gotten too close to the babies."

"Wow . . . learned something, eh, Rufus?"

They both smiled, relieved that he was back with them.

"Maybe we should fix the leash," she offered.

"Nah. I think he'll stay close now. C'mon, Rufe."

Martin's hunch was right: as they strolled farther along the path, Rufus showed no interest in leaving them this time. And within ten minutes they were like three old friends again, merrily strolling through the woods without a care. Martin talked more than he ever had in his life, providing the full scientific details on many of the rocks, trees, and bugs they came across along the way. Audrey seemed interested for a while, though eventually her attention started to wander a little.

When she stopped for a moment to jot down another note on her little pad, Martin gave her a curious look.

"What's your novel about?"

"Oh, the usual stuff. . . . Life. Love. Passion. The condition of man."

"Sounds fun. . . . When do you think you'll finish it?"

"Mm, well . . . technically I haven't started it yet. But I'm very close!"

Martin grinned, and they strolled along in comfortable silence.

Rufus, meanwhile, had calmed down quite a bit, and seemed content to tag along with them, sniffing around in the brush as they went. But when a gopher made the bad decision to dart across the path in front of them, Rufus—with a quick narrowing of the eyes, a flash of teeth, and a ferocious grunt—was on it in an instant. No clumsy miss this time; just like that, the furry rodent had become an afternoon snack.

"Wow!" Audrey said. "Did you see that?"

"He's quick."

"Doesn't this guy ever stop eating? He's like a vacuum cleaner."

"He needs it. He's growing so fast." He noticed Audrey chewing on her lower lip. "What."

"I feel sorry for the gopher."

"Yeah . . . that's the thing about nature. You've got your food chain, and at the bottom it's your first trophic level, like photosynthesizing plankton—"

"Hey, Martin? Do you think you could, kind of, like, dial it back a little with the science talk? I mean, it's cool and everything, but I think my head might explode."

"Oh. Okay." It hadn't occurred to him that she might be getting bored.

They stood there quietly; then Martin realized they weren't far from one of his favorite places in the woods.

"Last one to Munson Creek is an extinct species."

He suddenly took off down the footpath, and Audrey—not one to shrink from a challenge—darted after him. At first Rufus just watched them go with a vacant stare—but then, having no intention of being left alone again, he dashed after them.

They soon got to Munson Creek, and Martin and Audrey giggled as they raced down the slope to the stream bed. Martin vaulted across the creek and dove into a big, soft pile of dry leaves, nicely preserved from the past fall. Two seconds later, Audrey did the same.

"I win!" he hollered as they tossed big handfuls of leaves at each other, laughing and giggling like . . . well, like eleven-year-olds playing in a pile of leaves. Then Rufus charged into the creek, lost his footing on a slippery stone, and plopped face-first into the leaf pile, right next to them.

"Rufus, you lose!" cried Audrey, and she and Martin threw big gobs of leaves all over him. Excited by all the horseplay, he chomped down on a thick stick and swung it around in the air. Martin grabbed the other end, and the two of them wrestled for it as though Rufus were a frisky Labrador retriever.

"I think you feed him too much Fido-Nummy," Audrey said.

Martin got the stick loose from Rufus's jaws and tossed it across the creek. "Fetch, Rufus!" Rufus completely ignored the command.

"By the way, how do you know he's a he?" she asked.

"Mmm . . . just guessing, really." He spotted

something yellow right next to where the stick had landed, and went over to investigate. There, half buried in the dirt, was an old Frisbee. He pulled it out, brushed it off, and got an idea.

"I bet I can teach him a trick."

Audrey watched skeptically as Martin went into a half crouch and took aim.

"Rufus . . . Rufus! Catch!"

He reached back and gave the Frisbee a backhanded fling. His aim was perfect—but Rufus just stood there, barely even noticing as the plastic disk floated over and bounced off his chest.

"That's good, Martin. I'll call Eyewitness News."

"He needs practice."

He retrieved the Frisbee and took it back over to launching position. Meanwhile, Audrey's gaze wandered over to a low-hanging cloud. Something was on her mind.

As he took aim again, she asked the Dreaded Question.

"What are you gonna do when he gets *really* big?"

"Rufus! Catch!"

He flung the disk again, and this time it whizzed right past Rufus's head. He watched it fly by, but made no move to catch it.

Martin went to get it again.

"Sooner or later he won't fit in that barn anymore," Audrey said. "People will find out."

"It's not a big deal. There's still lots of time to think of something."

"Maybe if you told somebody now, there wouldn't be—"

"Rufus! See? Here it comes, boy. Ready? . . . Catch!"

He let the Frisbee fly once more, and this time it floated straight at Rufus's head—and with perfect timing, he snapped it right out of the air, instantly crushing it in his powerful jaws.

"Yeah!" Martin cried.

Rufus chewed on the yellow disk for a few seconds—until he realized that dirty plastic makes for a foul-tasting meal, and, with a dramatic gag, spat it out.

"This," Audrey declared, "is going to be a very weird summer."

# NINE

Twenty minutes later Audrey remembered that she still hadn't called Jade, and they headed for home. It had been a fun hour out there, especially for Rufus, and on the way back he was on his best behavior—he stayed close to Martin and Audrey and didn't make any more mad dashes at small animals. But they had a close call when, with perfectly bad timing, he managed to come down with a case of the hiccups.

As they learned at that moment, when a young T. rex gets the hiccups, it makes a very odd sound—sort of like a parrot imitating a toad's croak. Martin and Audrey might have thought it was funny at any other time, but when they spotted a pair of fishermen crossing through the woods about fifty yards away, they gasped and quickly ducked behind a rock, pulling Rufus down there with them. But Rufus kept hiccupping, and when the men heard the strange *blork!* echoing through the trees, they stopped to listen and look.

Martin tried to cover Rufus's mouth with his hand—not a very practical strategy, or a particularly smart one, considering the sharpness of Rufus's teeth.

*Blork!*

Martin and Audrey held their breath. Martin peeked out and saw the fishermen looking right in their direction, listening intently.

Finally, one of the men mumbled something to the other, and they continued on their way. Martin and Audrey breathed again. The secret stayed safe for now, but when she threw him a look, he knew exactly what she was thinking: fun or not, maybe this outing hadn't been such a great idea.

When they finally arrived back at the yard and headed for the barn, they heard the phone ringing in the house.

"That's probably my mom," Martin said, remembering he was supposed to have called her right after school. "Wait here."

He ran across the yard toward the house, not stopping to think that Rufus would try to follow him.

"Whoa!" Audrey yelped, grabbing the charging beast around the midsection. "Martin!"

Martin turned back to them but didn't stop. "Rufus, stay with Audrey. *Stay.*"

"You can't be serious."

"I'll bring my phone. Just hold him. I've gotta get this."

"Martin, wait! Ai-yai-yai . . ."

She struggled to hold on as Martin ran inside the house through the back door.

He raced across the kitchen and into the dining room.

"Hello?" he said, grabbing the phone on a small table against the wall. "Oh, um . . . she's not here right now. . . . Okay. Bye."

He trotted back into the kitchen, grabbed his backpack from the counter, and dug around for his forgotten cell phone. Once he had it, he stepped over and threw open the back door, but the instant he opened it—*splat!* Rufus leaped in like an eager puppy and landed on top of him, and they both crashed to the floor.

"What are you doing, you big doof?!"

Audrey ran through the door right behind him, eyes like poached eggs. "I couldn't hold him! He's too big!"

"You can't come in here, Rufus. Let's go. Out."

He started to lead Rufus back out the door—but again, Mother Nature had other ideas: a big horsefly with an obviously poor sense of direction buzzed right through the open door and into the kitchen. Rufus went after it.

"Hey!" Audrey and Martin shouted in unison.

The fly shot out into the dining room, and Rufus followed at full gallop.

"Ai-yai-yai-yai-yai," Audrey spluttered as she and Martin chased after him.

Rufus followed the pesky bug into the living room, trying to snap it out of midair. He ran all around the room, jumping on and off the furniture.

"What are you doing, you crazy dino?!" said Martin as he and Audrey scurried around after him, trying to grab him. When his tail whacked Mrs. Tinker's favorite lamp, Martin made a heroic lunge and righted it before it could topple to the floor.

"Will you keep *still*?" Audrey pleaded.

The fly buzzed off into the hall, and Martin decided to lay down the law. When Rufus sprinted for the hallway door, Martin jumped over and pushed his hands and feet up against the sides of the jamb, blocking the way.

"Rufus T. Rex, you stop running this instant!"

Rufus stopped in his tracks. He looked at Martin with curious eyes, panting from the chase but seeming in a calmer state now that the fly was out of sight.

"Now come with me."

Martin stepped in and motioned for Rufus to follow him to the kitchen. But unfortunately, no one had told the horsefly that the chase was over; it zipped into the room, did a quick circle, and zoomed right back out into the hall.

Rufus slipped past Martin and bolted after it again.

"No!" Martin cried as the wily bug whizzed into the den and Rufus followed.

As he and Audrey reached the den door, Martin

got an idea. "Go in and shut the door. I'll get some-thing."

"Get what?"

"Just do it!"

With a dull groan, Audrey went into the den and closed the door behind her. Meanwhile, Martin raced into the kitchen and threw open the fridge. He wasn't quite sure what he was looking for, but he knew it when he saw it: a package of raw pork chops, neatly wrapped in plastic on a Styrofoam tray.

He snatched up the chops and hustled back toward the den. But on his way there, he glanced out the liv-ing room window and froze solid: his mom had just gotten out of her car and was heading up the front walk.

"Ohhhhhhhh," Martin muttered. "This . . . is not a positive development."

Fighting his growing panic, he raced back to the den and threw open the door. Rufus wasn't focused on the fly anymore, because now he was chewing on a throw pillow. Audrey grabbed the other end and tried to pull it away from him, and they got into a tug-of-war.

"Little help here?!"

"My mom's home!"

She froze. "What? She just called you!"

"It wasn't her."

She gulped loudly.

Martin did some fast thinking. He ran over to the

window; Audrey followed, and they tried to pull it open. Nope—stuck like a barnacle on a boat hull.

Rufus caught a glimpse of the package in Martin's hand, took a couple of sniffs—and lunged straight at it. Martin snatched it away and went into all kinds of contortions to keep it away from Rufus's eager jaws. He tossed it to Audrey; when Rufus charged her, she tossed it back.

They both flinched at the sound of the front door slamming. "Martin!" His mom did not sound happy.

Martin quickly slipped out of the den and shut the door behind him. Suddenly remembering the pork chops in his hand, he swung the package behind his back and turned to greet his mom just as she came around the corner.

"Hi, Mom!" The smile was phony, but it was the best he could do.

"Martin," she snapped, "why didn't you call? Holy geez, I kept calling your cell, I called the house, then I thought maybe you went to work after all, so I called your dad and *he* hadn't seen you, and that got me all worried, so I had to leave work early, and now I'm going to have to—"

There was a *squawk* and a *thump* in the den.

"*What* is that *noise*?"

"Noise? . . . Oh, um . . . I have a friend over."

"Well, if you're going to— What? . . . Really?" Just like that, her anger vanished. "Well, gosh, Martin. Let me meet him."

She reached for the den doorknob, but he quickly stepped in front of her.

"No! Um . . . I mean . . . not right now, because . . . uh . . ."

He knew he needed to finish that sentence, but his mind was an empty vessel.

He was saved when the door opened—just a crack so nobody could see inside—and Audrey's smiling face appeared.

"Hello."

Now his mom was smiling too. "Hi!" she said as Audrey slipped through the door and shut it behind her. "I'm Martin's mom. Who are you?"

"Audrey Blanchard."

"Pleased to meet you, Audrey."

As they stiffly shook hands, there was a *crash* and another *squawk* from inside the den.

Mrs. Tinker looked fully perplexed. "Martin, what on *earth*?"

"That's, uh . . . the TV. We're watching a monster movie."

"A little loud, don't you think?"

"He's destroying New York."

"Well, turn it down, honey. It's too loud."

"Okay."

The three of them stood there silently for a few seconds as his mom just smiled. Martin turned to Audrey.

"Weren't you gonna call your sister?"

"Hmm? . . . Oh! Right." She put on her polite face

and spoke to Mrs. Tinker. "Can I please use your phone?"

"Sure."

Again, they all just stood there. Martin fidgeted, dreading another sound from the other side of the door.

"Could you . . . show me?" Audrey asked.

"Oh! Of course."

As Mrs. Tinker led Audrey toward the dining room, Martin let out a big breath and slipped back through the den door.

But his work wasn't done. Rufus was thrashing around with the pillow in his mouth, spreading the stuffing all over the place.

"Rufus!" he exclaimed in a loud whisper. "Look!" He waved the pork chops in the air, and Rufus dropped the pillow and went right after them. Martin was quick enough to keep the package just out of reach of those voracious jaws, and he used the lure to lead Rufus out into the hall and back toward the kitchen.

He could hear his mom talking to Audrey through the door to the dining room as she showed her the phone. "Would you like to stay for dinner? We'd love to have you join us."

"Oh, um . . . thank you. I'll ask."

Rufus was taking his sweet time getting into the kitchen, and Martin could hear his mom's footsteps coming back toward the hall. He could just see Audrey over at the phone, and he gestured to her frantically with his free hand.

"Ohmygosh!" Audrey said loudly. "What's that?"

Her sudden outburst turned Mrs. Tinker back around. "Hm?"

Audrey pointed out the front window. "Over there. Next to the, the . . . over there."

"What."

"Isn't that a . . . um . . . y'know, one of those *things* . . . ?"

"Where?"

With Mrs. Tinker distracted by the big nothing Audrey was pointing out, Martin was finally able to coax Rufus out of the hall and into the kitchen.

"Oh. Guess not," he could hear Audrey say, sounding much relieved. "Never mind."

Just when Martin thought he finally had it under control, Rufus jumped back into the hall to check out this new, larger human standing at the other end with her back to him. As Mrs. Tinker started to turn toward him . . .

*"Oh!"* Audrey yelped.

"Wha?" Startled, Martin's mom turned her back again, and it gave him just enough time to grab Rufus and pull him into the kitchen.

"Oh," Audrey said, much more calmly. "Oh, um . . . a crow. That's what it was."

"A crow," said Mrs. Tinker.

Martin figured by now his mom must have thought his new friend was a few ponies short of a polo team. But it was worth it if they could just make it a few more seconds and not get caught.

Finally, he managed to push Rufus out the kitchen door to the yard; then he used the pork chops to lead him all the way across to the far side of the barn.

"You are a bad, bad boy," he said as they scurried down the incline to the creaky wooden doors. "That's the last time you're coming out of there, *period.*"

He tossed the package into the cellar and, when Rufus dove in after it, closed the doors tightly behind him. He tipped against the door with a giant sigh. *This could get very challenging.*

Audrey caught an earful from Jade for taking so long to check in with her. But once Audrey explained about her first new friend since they moved there, her sister became much more agreeable and told Audrey it would be okay for her to stay at the Tinkers' for dinner.

The meal was a pleasant and polite occasion, though Martin's dad was his usual quiet, distracted self. Mrs. Tinker really seemed to like Audrey, and she couldn't stop smiling at the strange sight of Martin with a real, honest-to-goodness friend. Normally that might have made Martin uncomfortable, but the thought that he and Audrey were sharing this fantastic secret kept him in a cheerful frame of mind.

Martin's mom had lots of questions for Audrey, like how do you like Menominee Springs (it's pretty cool), what are your plans for the summer (get started on that novel), and where did you get that beautiful red hair (my dad picked it up for me at Walmart).

Mrs. Tinker got a laugh out of that last one. It was Audrey's standard joke when she was asked that.

When she had finished her last bite, Audrey placed her napkin neatly on the table. "That was very good, Mrs. Tinker."

"Thank you, Audrey! I'm really sorry it was just hot dogs and beans. I was sure I had some pork chops, but I don't know."

"That's okay. I like beans."

Trying to hide their urge to snicker, Martin and Audrey both took a drink of water.

"Oh, Gordy," Mrs. Tinker said, "I ran into Rufus today."

That did it: at exactly the same moment, two mouthfuls of water went airborne with a stereophonic *thphhhwwwww!* Mr. and Mrs. Tinker looked at them, unamused.

"Sorry," Martin said quietly, mopping up the wet spots with his napkin. "Got some down the wrong pipe."

"Me too," said Audrey. "Sorry."

Martin's dad went back to his baked beans. "What'd he say?"

"Not much, really," Mrs. Tinker said. "He wants to have us for dinner one of these days."

Again, Martin and Audrey couldn't hold back a giggle. "Rufus" having them for dinner? Too funny.

Mrs. Tinker half smiled, kind of like she wanted in on the joke. But Mr. Tinker failed to see the humor. The other Rufus was his brother, after all, and it sure seemed like these kids were making fun of him. "What's funny?" he asked coolly.

"Nothing," Martin said, working hard to flush the silliness off his face. "Can we be excused?"

There was a heavy pause as his mom and dad just looked at him. "Okay," Mrs. Tinker finally said.

Martin and Audrey scooped up their dishes, dropped them in the kitchen sink, and were out the back door in a flash.

Martin was pretty sure his dad was not exactly thrilled by this new friend of his. Not because she was unpleasant or she dressed kind of weird or anything like that, but because she was . . . well, a *she*. Dad surely would have preferred that Martin make a *guy* friend, somebody he could do *guy* things with, like building a tree fort and trading baseball cards and, yes, tossing a football around. Maybe if he were a little older, it would be a different story. But for now, he figured his mom would stick up for him, and eventually his dad would learn to roll with it. That was the way it usually went.

So, with summer under way and nothing but carefree thoughts in their heads, Martin and Audrey went back out to the barn to hang out, goof around, and keep Rufus company. It was to be the beginning of a *very* interesting three months.

# TEN

Audrey had had some friends when she lived in Oshkosh, but she struggled making new ones in Menominee Springs. She could never quite shake the "Tippi Tomato" label Donald had saddled her with, and the other girls sometimes teased her for her rather oddball fashion sense. And considering Martin's sad history in the friend-making department, it was perfectly natural that the two of them would get together. But they didn't just team up out of desperation; they really did enjoy each other's company.

They hung out together almost every day, and everybody started thinking of them as two peas in a pod. Every now and then they'd be seen together in town by other kids from school, who would snicker to each other, or even call out some snide comment like

"Marty and Tippi are *engaged,* wooooo!" But Audrey and Martin didn't really care; they were used to being teased, and besides, they were enjoying their summer vacation way too much to worry about it.

One of the things they enjoyed the most was going out to the barn, where they could work on Martin's collections, play Monopoly or Twenty Questions or phone app games, do a little light reading, just chat and joke around, or play with the pet dinosaur.

That was their favorite thing to do, because it seemed like Rufus was always surprising them with something new. Martin kept at it with the Frisbee lessons, and after a couple of weeks Rufus was actually able to catch it on a fairly consistent basis. Soon they were throwing other stuff to him too—sticks, a beat-up shoe, an old rubber hose, a tennis ball, and, of course, pieces of meat, which he hardly ever missed. But once he learned what was edible and what wasn't, he pretty much lost interest in catching anything but the meat.

He also seemed to enjoy a bit of horseplay with them now and then—the best way for him to get some exercise without leaving the barn, Martin figured. They played a game Martin called Blinko, where he would turn out the lights and then he and Audrey would each turn on a flashlight and shoot the beams all around the room. Rufus always ran himself ragged trying to catch the darting spots of light, and could never quite figure out why there was nothing there to bite into. Every now and then Audrey or Martin would yell "Blinko!"

and give his tail a yank, which got him even more dis-combobulated. But he did seem to understand, from the persistent giggles of his human companions, that it was all in good fun.

One time, though, Audrey got whacked in the face with that flying tail. So that pretty much ended the Blinko games.

Another thing they enjoyed was to take turns with Martin's phone camera shooting pictures of each other in silly poses with Rufus—like Audrey kissing him on the snout, or Martin putting a funny hat on his head and dancing a stumbly waltz with him around the cellar floor. Martin wasn't supposed to use his dad's computer (he usually took it with him to work anyway), so they would head over to Audrey's place when nobody was home and print out the pictures—then have a good laugh at the wacky scenes they'd created.

And the pictures kept getting wackier, because Rufus kept getting bigger.

Martin dutifully kept his chart up to date:

| WEEK | LENGTH (nose to tail) | HEIGHT | GIRTH (belly) | WEIGHT (approx.) |
|------|------------|--------|-------|--------|
| Week 6 | 5 ft. 4 in. | 4 ft. 1 in. | 26 in. | 84 lb. |
| Week 7 | 6 ft. 0 in. | 4 ft. 4 in. | 28 in. | 106 lb. |
| Week 8 | 6 ft. 8 in. | 4 ft. 7 in. | 31 in. | 133 lb. |
| Week 9 | 7 ft. 3 in. | 4 ft. 10 in. | 34 in. | 161 lb. |
| Week 10 | 7 ft. 11 in. | 5 ft. 2 in. | 36 in. | 188 lb. |

Martin was usually able to get Rufus close enough to a wall to make a pretty accurate height mark, and stretching a tape measure around his belly wasn't too hard with Audrey's help. But they had to measure the length when Rufus was asleep, because he wouldn't sit still long enough for them to stretch the tape from one end to the other.

His skin darkened and hardened as he grew, the scales taking on a rather rough texture, like elephant skin. He also made a lot of different sounds; it seemed like he added a new one every day. Soon he had a whole inventory of bleats, blorks, sniffs, snorts, growls, yowls, and grumbles, and in an hour's time you might hear every one of them. Martin figured there must have been some sophisticated dino language going on there, though he didn't have a clue what any of it meant. Maybe with time he could figure it out.

And, of course, there were those ever-growing teeth—exactly fifty-two long, curved, pearly daggers, getting longer every day.

Feeding him got to be more and more of a problem. Martin kept putting in a few hours at the Trout Palace on most mornings, and he spent pretty much all his earnings on big bags of Fido-Nummy—the small cans just weren't enough anymore. He had to be careful not to always get them at the same store, and not to go to the same checkout clerk too many times, because he didn't want anybody to start asking questions. Sometimes Audrey went with him, and she would help out by taking a bag to a different checkout stand.

But as time went on, it got harder and harder to keep Rufus well fed with just the dog food. By the end of June he was eating five pounds of Fido-Nummy every day—but he always wanted more. So Martin and Audrey had to get creative to find other stuff for him to eat. Sometimes Martin would sneak into the kitchen of the Heart o' the Woods restaurant, pretending he was there to sweep the floor, and gather up table scraps and leftovers before they could be thrown out. Audrey did her part too, making friends with the butchers at the Food Bear, and making off with whatever remnants they could spare (for her Great Dane, she told them).

The kids found they didn't have to be too picky with what they fed to Rufus. He would eat pretty much anything, as long as it was either alive or had been recently.

Every year the town had a big Fourth of July barbecue on the village commons, and this year Audrey and Martin used the occasion to round up a hefty haul of dino chow. As it happened, the grill master was the person Martin least wanted to talk to—Sheriff Frank Grimes. When Martin stepped up to the grill with an open bun for the fourth time, the sheriff couldn't hide his astonishment.

"Hoho, whoa there, dude! What's that, about five for you, Martin?"

"I like hot dogs."

"For a little squirt, you sure can put 'em away, eh? Ha ha ha! Here y'go."

Each time, Audrey was right behind Martin in line.

"You too, Matilda? We're gonna have to roll the two of you out of here like beach balls. Haaaa ha ha ha!"

But they weren't eating the hot dogs. When nobody was watching, they dropped the wieners into plastic bags and tucked them away in Martin's backpack. They also wandered around the park, furtively scooping up stray pieces of burger and hot dog left behind by other picnickers.

It wasn't the most sanitary way to spend a holiday afternoon, but for Martin and Audrey there was an odd kind of fun to it—like they were pulling off a well-planned bank robbery together. Best of all, by the end of the day they had racked up an impressive stash of meaty morsels to take home and feed to Rufus.

Rufus had no way of knowing where this mouth-watering feast came from, but he had no hesitation about wolfing it down. To Martin's and Audrey's amazement, he polished off the wieners and burgers in no time at all.

"When does he ever quit?" Audrey asked in exasperation, and Martin had no answer but a sigh and a shrug. This was getting to be a lot of work.

Then again, what did he expect from a creature that couldn't stop growing *bigger*?

\* \* \*

It wasn't as much fun as hanging out in the barn, but sometimes they would spend the afternoon at Audrey's house. Martin was glad he finally got to meet her dad and her sister, Jade, and those two seemed just as delighted as Mrs. Tinker that Martin and Audrey had become friends. Mr. Blanchard (or J.B., as he liked to be called) and Jade were especially nice to Martin, and he liked that.

They had Martin over for dinner a few times, and that was fun, but the best day was when J.B. took the two girls and Martin up to Lake Manitowish to do some fishing. Martin had never gone out fishing on a boat before; his dad had been promising to take him for years but hadn't quite gotten around to it.

It turned out J.B. was something of an expert, and the girls knew a thing or two about it too. So Martin got a full lesson on the best ways to catch trout, muskie, perch, walleye, crappie, and, of course, the largemouth bass.

As it turned out, the trout were really biting that day. Among the four of them they caught nine fish, three of which were big enough to keep. J.B. and Jade wanted to throw them back anyway—but Audrey and Martin insisted on keeping them. So into the ice chest went the fish for the long drive home.

Martin told J.B. that his plan was to have the fish stuffed so he could hang them on his bedroom wall. The real story, of course, was a bit more interesting.

After all, back at the barn, there was a very large

mouth to feed, and it wasn't a bass. And it kept on getting bigger.

Besides the problem of keeping Rufus fed, it got to be an ever-bigger challenge for Martin and Audrey to keep him happy in that barn cellar. As the summer went on, he got more and more restless down there. And as he grew, somehow the room didn't seem so big anymore. It was also starting to smell a bit like the monkey house at the zoo, even though Martin kept on shoveling up those growing piles of dinosaur poop. He finally started buying some baking soda to sprinkle around, and that helped a bit.

Rufus also got lonely when the kids weren't there. He would pace back and forth like a caged tiger, or try to climb up a wall to get to those high windows that provided light but only a narrow and distant view of the outside world. Martin and Audrey did their best to keep him entertained, but he eventually lost interest in the silly games they used to play together. Martin even tried to get the Blinko going again, but Rufus just couldn't seem to get that interested.

"I guess he's getting too old for this stuff," Martin said to Audrey. But they both knew there was more to it than that. Sometimes Rufus would try to push his way through the double doors as the kids came in from outside, or scratch at the doors with his tiny front claws. Martin tried to discourage this behavior by giving Rufus a little smack on the snout, then wagging a finger in his face. But somehow Rufus never seemed to get the message.

Though neither of them dared to bring up the subject, Martin knew that they wouldn't be able to keep their secret forever. But for now Lady Luck stayed on their side, because nobody else ever ventured near that barn. Well, except once.

Martin had convinced his dad that he was old enough to mow the lawn and do odd yard work for extra cash (more Fido-Nummy!). But on one especially nice afternoon in August, Martin's mom decided she wanted to prune the rosebushes herself—and some of those bushes were right alongside the barn.

When Martin arrived home from the Trout Palace, he stepped into the yard and spotted her working her way along the wall, snipping and snapping. He froze in horror as she stooped down right in front of one of those cellar windows. Somehow she didn't notice when a large, scaly face appeared on the other side of the glass, eyeballing her with intense curiosity, his moist breath making silvery puffs on the pane.

Discovering muscles in his legs he never knew he possessed, Martin shot across the yard and inserted himself between his mom and the cellar window.

"Mom! Hi."

"What's up, doodlebug?"

"What are you doing here?"

"I live here."

"I mean, you're . . . shouldn't you be at work?"

"Not on Sunday. Beautiful day to be out, huh?"

"I can do this. Why don't you go in and relax?"

"I am relaxed. Don't you love this fresh air?"

"But the sun is so hot, and you know how easily you burn. And the *bugs*. Wow. You *really* hate bugs."

His mom gave him a squinty look, then stood up and plunked the pruning shears into his hand. "All right, Martin. If you're so keen on it, be my guest."

He threw her a phony smile as she turned and headed for the house, not noticing that a toothy reptile was bobbing his head back and forth in the window behind Martin. Rufus also started making chirping noises, which stopped her in her tracks.

"What?" she said, turning back.

Martin launched into a fit of fake coughing, neatly drowning out Rufus's muffled squeals.

"Are you okay?"

"I swallowed a gnat or something. See what I mean? Bugs."

With a few more coughs to cap off the performance, he turned around and went to work on a rosebush, hoping she would take it as a cue to go inside, which, luckily, she did.

That was the closest either one of his parents came to discovering Rufus the whole summer. As for his dad, well, he was hardly ever home; and when he did make an appearance, he was usually crashed out in his reclining chair, watching a Brewers game or a *CSI: Miami* rerun, exhausted from a long day of repairing a lot of rickety old equipment that Ben

Fairfield refused to replace. Every now and then Martin and Audrey spotted him watching them through a window, or sometimes he would just give them a vaguely disapproving glance before walking by. Audrey figured he didn't like her very much, but Martin explained that it was nothing personal, just the thing about her being a girl and all.

That wasn't their biggest concern, though; there was this other, growing problem to be thinking about.

| WEEK | LENGTH (nose to tail) | HEIGHT | GIRTH (belly) | WEIGHT (approx.) |
|---|---|---|---|---|
| Week 11 | 8 ft. 7 in. | 5 ft. 4 in. | 39 in. | 215 lb. |
| Week 12 | 9 ft. 2 in. | 5 ft. 6 in.? | 41 in. | 250 lb.? |
| Week 13 | 9 ft. 9 in. | 5 ft. 10 in.? | 43 in. | 275 lb.? |
| Week 14 | 10 ft. 3 in. | 6 ft. 1 in.? | 45 in. | 300 lb.? |
| Week 15 | 10 ft. 10 in. | 6 ft. 4 in.? | 46 in. | 325 lb.? |
| Week 16 | 11 ft. 5 in. | 6 ft. 7 in.? | 48 in. | 350 lb.? |
| Week 17 | 12 ft. 0 in. | 6 ft. 11 in.? | 49 in. | 375 lb.? |
| Week 18 | 12 ft. 8 in. | 7 ft. 1 in.? | 50 in. | 400 lb.? |

It got harder and harder for Martin and Audrey to measure Rufus's height, because they couldn't reach the measuring stick from his head to the wall. So Martin got on a chair and measured seven feet three inches from the floor to a ceiling beam; by late August, he could see that Rufus was just a few inches below the beam when he stood up straight. As for the weight, that got to be pure guesswork; getting his big friend on the scale became flat-out impossible.

And then there were those growing teeth. An inch and a half, two inches, two and a half inches and counting . . . and sharp as ice picks. Where would it end?

Any way you looked at it, there was just no stopping this guy from getting confoundingly, exhaustingly, bewilderingly BIGGER.


In what seemed like a flash, summer started winding down, and Labor Day was just around the corner. Soon school would be starting up again, the leaves would start falling, and the Trout Palace would close down until the spring. Somehow Martin and Audrey had made it through the summer without Rufus being discovered or—worse—escaping from the barn. All in all, things had gone pretty well. Maybe a bit *too* well.

On a warm, windless, late summer night, Martin tossed around in his bed. The window was open, and now, mixed in with the usual cricket sounds, some strange noises were wafting up from the far end of the yard.

Rufus had gotten in the habit of pacing around the barn cellar at night, making strange bleating noises along with an occasional screechy howl.

*Eeh eeh eeh eeh! Howooooo . . .*

Before, the barn walls had done a pretty good job of holding the sounds in. But Rufus's noises got louder as he grew, and now the racket was starting to travel all the way up to the house.

Martin was trying hard not to let it bother him—but the harder he tried, the more bothered he got. Deciding a short hike to the bathroom might help calm his nerves, he sprang out of bed and headed into the hall.

Unfortunately, the trip didn't relieve anything other than his bladder.

On his way back, he stopped at his parents' bedroom door and peeked through the keyhole. Their window was open too, and that same haunting noise kept drifting up from below.

*Eeh eeh eeh eeh! Howooooooo . . . Eeh eeh eeh eeh eeh!*

Dad seemed to be sleeping through it, but Mom was restless like Martin—the sandman had obviously abandoned her, too.

She reached over and gave Mr. Tinker a vigorous shake. "Gord."

"Mmnh."

"You awake?"

"No."

"Do you hear that?"

"What."

"Sounds like a wolf."

With a hollow groan, Mr. Tinker rolled over to take a listen.

"Just a bird. Go back to sleep," he mumbled, and rolled back into his snoozing posture.

Mrs. Tinker listened for a while longer, then rolled the other way and pulled the pillow tightly over her head.

Martin let out a long breath, then tiptoed back to his room and slipped into bed. He lay there stiffly, staring up at the ceiling, eyes wide open, palms sweating, stomach churning. Much as he hated thinking about it, he knew that before long the best summer of his life would be a distant memory. Something was going to happen soon, and it was not going to be good.

That's generally the way it goes if you're keeping a pet dinosaur, and the darned thing just keeps on getting maddeningly, thrillingly, scarily, nerve-rackingly, uncontrollably, mind-bogglingly—

Well, you know.

# ELEVEN

**O**ver the course of the summer, Martin had been spending more and more time at the Trout Palace, working three or even four hours in the mornings and early afternoons, doing those odd jobs for a handful of dollars a day. He didn't particularly enjoy it, but—well, he *needed* those dollars. He had growing *obligations.*

Since Martin wasn't an "official" employee, Mr. Fairfield kept giving Mr. Tinker a bit of extra cash each week to pass on to Martin. The arrangement was basically a favor that Mr. Fairfield was doing for Mr. Tinker, his most valued employee.

But business was not very good at the Trout Palace that summer, so Ben Fairfield's moods had gotten more and more sour as time went on. It made Martin especially nervous when Mr. Fairfield would watch him as he worked, a stony expression on his face.

One late August day, as Martin was running an electric weed trimmer around the edges of the Walleye Theater, he spotted Mr. Fairfield talking sternly to his dad. He pretended not to notice, but suspected the worst when their talk ended and his dad immediately strode up behind him.

"Martin . . . Marty!"

He let out a whistle, and Martin shut off the trimmer.

"What time did you come in today?"

"About nine, I guess."

"You been working this whole time?"

Sensing where this was going, Martin gave a half nod.

His dad adopted a tone kind of like one of those old-time TV dads, understanding yet firm. "Look, son. I'm glad you've got this work ethic and all. But here's the deal: you're costing us too much money, okay? Plus, Ben is afraid somebody's gonna call the labor board on him. He wanted to cut you loose altogether, but I talked him into keeping you on till we close, end of next month. From now on, though, you can only do an hour a day, tops. Got it?"

Martin fidgeted, looked around, and tried to think of a good comeback. But, as usual at times like this, his brain froze.

"You won't have the time for it once school starts, anyway."

Martin glanced around nervously, as though looking for something to reassure him.

His expression softening, Mr. Tinker reached into his wallet and pulled out a few bills.

"Here y'go. I'll, um . . . I'll bring you an ice cream or something later, okay?"

Martin nodded vaguely and reached for the greenbacks, but his dad pulled them back.

"What've you been doing with all this money, anyway?"

"Oh . . . um. Saving it."

"For what?"

"Stuff like . . . y'know . . . the future."

Before his dad could wrap his brain around that one, Martin snatched the bills and, with a half-mumbled "Thanks," headed on his way.


"Martin, we have to talk about this *now,*" Audrey said as they pulled a bag of Fido-Nummy from the shelf at the Food Bear, letting it fall noisily into their cart. "If we don't do something soon, things are going to turn very bad."

"How do you know?"

"Because I know."

"We don't have to be in any big rush."

"He keeps needing more and more, and we can't afford it. And now that you're laid off—"

"I am not laid off. It's an hours cutback."

"He's getting too big! And you know how he hates being stuck in that barn."

Martin groaned under his breath. It was the best he could do, because he didn't have a good answer for her.

"And school starts up next week. What are we supposed to do then?"

"So what are you saying? You think we should just *let him go*?"

"No, dummy. I'm just saying we have to, you know . . . *tell* somebody."

"Like who?"

"Like who? Well . . . okay. I think if we tell . . . um . . . your parents—"

"Noooo, no, no, no . . ."

"Why not?"

"They'll just send him away, and he'll end up in a cage somewhere. And I'll probably get grounded for life."

"Don't you think they'll find out sooner or later anyway?"

"I'm not telling my parents!"

"Shhhhh!"

The conversation had gotten kind of loud, and people were throwing glances their way.

Audrey took a deep breath and let it out in a long *whoooooph*. "Okay then . . . we could start with Jade. I know I can trust her—"

"Ohhhhh . . ."

"Then we could all go to *my* dad—"

"No, that's no good."

"Martin, we have to tell somebody! The longer we put it off, the worse it's gonna be when they find out."

"I'm not against telling, it just . . . has to be the right person."

"Okay, so who?"

"Somebody who can make sure he gets treated well. Somebody we can trust to not just sell him or something."

"Do you know anybody like that?"

Martin had actually thought about that question quite a bit. And the answer he kept coming up with, sad to say, was no.

Seventh grade, to no one's surprise, turned out to be a lot like sixth, except now it was Mrs. Sanders instead of Ms. Olerud, and room 13B instead of room 11A. And it was the same bunch of kids, which most of them were happy about, but not Martin. All he had to look forward to was another long year of being ignored, then picked on, then ignored again, then picked on again. Maybe, he hoped, eighth grade would be better. But probably not.

One good thing, though, was that Mr. Eckhart was the science teacher again. Martin had always hoped that somehow he might turn out like Mr. Eckhart when he grew up—really smart about science, but at the same time kind of a cool guy. Mr. Eckhart was living proof that it was actually possible to be both.

On the second day of school, everybody was assigned to present something interesting about science in front of the class. Donald Grimes, thinking himself an expert on a lot of things, led off by banging two plastic toy dinosaurs against each other, making all kinds of gruesome sound effects as though it were a dramatic fight to the death.

A lot of the kids laughed, which only encouraged Donald to ham it up even more. After a good half minute or so of his goofy melodrama, he held up one of the dino toys.

"Brontosaurus," he stated with authority. "Also known as . . ." His face went blank. "Something with an *A* . . ."

"Anybody know?" said Mr. Eckhart.

"Apatosaurus," Martin said without hesitating.

Donald threw him a chilly glance. "Aptapottosaurus," he said. "This was one big mother dino. I mean *big*. Got its food by stomping on other dinosaurs."

"It did not," Martin interjected. "It was a plant eater."

"Do you mind, Tinker? This is *my* report."

"You're telling it wrong."

Normally Martin wouldn't challenge Donald like that, but . . . well, he was getting it all messed up. Somebody had to say something.

"It's all right, Martin," Mr. Eckhart said. "Let him do it."

Donald put down the apatosaurus and picked up one of his other props. "This one is called tri . . . tri . . ." He glanced at Mr. Eckhart for a hint, but all he got was a nod of encouragement. "Tricycle tops?"

"Triceratops," Mr. Eckhart corrected him.

"Triceratops," Donald said, as though he had known it all along. "Why is it called by this name? We can only guess. The point is, this baby was *mean*. How do we know? Well, *geez*. Look at the horns on that sucker. Arr, arrr, *arrr!*"

He jabbed the little dino in the air a few times like a knife, and the class couldn't help but giggle. Martin and Audrey just exchanged dismissive smirks.

Donald put down the triceratops and picked up one more toy, ready for his big finish.

"Tyrannosaurus rex," he said dramatically. "Most vicious, nasty, rotten monster that ever lived. You get near one of these babies . . . you're lunch meat." He jammed the little dino's teeth into his neck and staggered around, emitting unearthly yowls of pain. The class broke out in a loud chorus of laughter.

It was more than Martin could take. "That's stupid!" he shouted, even louder than the laughers. Suddenly, everybody went quiet and looked at him.

"They weren't mean," he stated with authority. "They were loyal and friendly. You just had to know how to treat them."

"Shut your yap, Tinker!" Donald snapped. "How would you know?"

"All right, all right," Mr. Eckhart interjected.

"Truth is, we're not sure what they were really like. Is the show over, Donald?"

Still scowling, Donald gathered up his props. On the way back to his seat, he shot Martin a withering look.

Martin knew there would be a price to pay later, but for now he just tried to ignore Donald's frosty glare. Then he noticed something out of the corner of his eye and looked over to see Audrey excitedly waving her hands at him and mouthing something he couldn't make out.

"Hey, Marty," said Nate Stoller, "your wife is calling you." The class cracked up, and Audrey shrank back into her seat.

Mr. Eckhart cleared his throat loudly, quieting everybody down.

"Okay! Who's next?"

The school day was over an hour later; kids crowded into the halls, as usual, and Martin made his customary trudge toward his locker. But he didn't get very far before Audrey came running up behind him. "Martin, wait up!"

"Hi."

"Are you thinking what I'm thinking?"

"No. What?"

She leaned in and whispered intently. "Mr. Eckhart!"

"What about him?"

"He's the one we can tell, dodo!"

"What? No."

"Why not? He's the perfect one. If anybody would make sure Rufus got treated well, it's him. He would help us, and we wouldn't get in trouble."

"How do you know?"

She gave an impatient grunt. "I *know,* okay? Martin, you know I'm right. We *have* to do it!"

"Okay, okay," Martin said tautly, trying to quiet her down. "Maybe on . . . Thursday, we can—"

"No! Today! Now!"

"Really?"

"I've got the pictures in my locker. Come on."

Suddenly, a familiar gravelly voice thundered from down the hall. "Hey! Tinkywinks!" Donald Grimes fired up his feet and charged toward them. He was not smiling.

"Meet me at his office," Martin said hurriedly to Audrey as he took off down the hall ahead of his fast-approaching tormentor.

"Try and make me look bad, you little phlegm-wad," Donald growled as he chugged after him. But the chase didn't last long; as Donald sped past Audrey, she casually stuck out her foot, catching him just above the left ankle and sending him sprawling onto the freshly waxed floor. Martin peeked back around the corner to see Donald skidding like a penguin on an ice floe, headfirst, sliding a good ten feet. He would have gone even farther if his forehead hadn't made a direct hit on the shin of the school principal, Mr. Clayborne.

Mr. Clayborne was *not* somebody you wanted to mess with. He was well known for running a tight ship, and horseplay in the halls was one of his very top pet peeves.

Donald looked up at the scowling face six feet above him, and all he could manage was a pained, innocent grin.

Audrey, meanwhile, slipped away and headed straight for her locker.

When Audrey and Martin arrived at Mr. Eckhart's tiny, cluttered office, he was busy packing his brief-case. He was obviously in a hurry, and barely glanced at them as they timidly stepped through the door.

"Hi, guys," he mumbled.

He didn't stop what he was doing, and Martin, thinking it must be a bad time, couldn't get the words flowing. Audrey gave him a firm elbow nudge, and that did the trick.

"Mr. Eckhart . . . can we talk to you for a minute?"

"I dunno, Martin. I'm overdue at the U." The U was the university down the road in Granville, where his graduate studies kept him busy when he wasn't teaching.

"It's really, *really* important," said Audrey.

Mr. Eckhart still didn't look at them. "What's up?"

Martin braced himself for the big announcement. "Um . . . remember when I asked you about lizards with three toes?"

"Yeah. Glasses. Where the heck did I . . . ?"

"What if I told you I have one that's seven feet tall?"

"Really?" said Mr. Eckhart dully, still not paying attention.

"It's a dinosaur, Mr. Eckhart," said Audrey.

"Tyrannosaurus rex," said Martin.

"Mm-hm," said Mr. Eckhart, and a few seconds later it finally registered. He stopped what he was doing and looked at the two of them, one eyebrow up and mouth pinched to the side.

"I found this egg, and it hatched and he grew up. Well, he's *growing* up."

"And no one else knows about him," Audrey said, "but now he's too big for that stupid barn and we had to tell somebody."

"And we wanted it to be you," Martin added quickly, "because you would know the best thing to do with a dinosaur."

Mr. Eckhart's eyes shifted back and forth between them, his face frozen in a twisted frown. They returned his gaze nervously for what seemed to Martin like about an hour and a half. Finally, the sides of his mouth turned up ever so slightly.

"Okay, I get it. You two are funnier than I gave you credit for."

"It's not a joke!" Audrey insisted.

"I know it sounds crazy," said Martin, "but it's true, I swear!"

Mr. Eckhart resumed throwing papers into his

briefcase. "Look, I don't know what you two are up to, but right now I do not—"

Audrey shoved a handful of papers in front of his face—the color printouts of the photos they had taken with Rufus.

As Mr. Eckhart took them and glanced through the first two or three, his face went through a whole series of vivid expressions that could have gotten him the lead in the school play. At first he seemed taken aback, but gradually a skeptical smirk took over.

"You guys are very good with Photoshop, I'll give you that."

"They're not fake," said Martin.

"We don't even have Photoshop," said Audrey. *"Look."*

Mr. Eckhart leafed through the rest of the photos, one by one. With each new picture he looked more and more confused, like he was doubting his own eyes.

# TWELVE

Mr. Eckhart called his colleague at the U to postpone their appointment, and as he drove Martin and Audrey to the Tinkers' house, Martin told him the whole story. But Mr. Eckhart didn't seem to be buying a word of it, and the disruption to his day put him in a bit of a testy mood.

"I'm here to tell you, Martin," he said as he followed the kids across the backyard, "a sixty-five-million-year-old egg does not just thaw out and hatch. If anybody should know that, it's you."

"When you see him, you'll believe it," Martin said. They rounded the far corner of the barn and climbed down the slope toward the double doors leading to the lower level.

"Well, if this turns into a punch line, there will be major detentions in your futures, both of you."

Suddenly, Audrey let out a gasp, and she and Martin stopped in their tracks. Mr. Eckhart almost ran into them from behind.

"Oh, no!" she moaned as they stared at the scene just ten feet in front of them: a pair of wooden barn doors, hanging wide open.

Martin and Audrey ran through the doors and into the barn cellar. "Rufus?" Martin called, hoping that his scaly friend would wander out from behind a pile of junk, like he usually did.

Not this time.

Audrey and Martin ran all around the lower barn room, frantically checking every nook and possible hiding place. But it didn't take long for the horrible truth to sink in. Martin ran over to check out the metal latch on the door, and saw that it had been chewed on by a set of very sharp teeth.

"Wow. I never thought he could do that."

They both ran back outside and called into the woods. "Rufus!" they shouted, nearly in unison. The silence that greeted them in return made Martin's stomach feel like an overloaded bug jar.

"This is very, very bad," said Audrey.

Mr. Eckhart was starting to twitch impatiently. "All right, look, you two—"

"We've gotta find him," said Martin, and in a flash he and Audrey were racing into the woods.

Mr. Eckhart put on his sternest voice. "Martin!" But, seeing that he was scolding the clear September air, all he could do was throw up his hands and follow them.

He halfheartedly tried to keep up as they scurried around, calling for Rufus in all directions. Audrey was a good whistler and she tried that, too—but all that came of their combined efforts was more of that disheartening silence.

"We better split up," said Martin.

What little was left of Mr. Eckhart's patience seemed to be pretty much spent. "Okay, just hold on one second here—"

"Could you please come with me, Mr. Eckhart?" Audrey interrupted. "I don't know these woods that well."

"Oh, and I do?"

"I'll feel safer. Please?"

His mouth was open, but his vocal cords were not serving him at the moment. Maybe he was thinking of tomorrow's headline: GIRL DISAPPEARS IN WOODS; TEACHER CHARGED WITH CHILD ABANDONMENT.

"I'll meet you guys at the white rock in twenty minutes," Martin said authoritatively.

"Okay," said Audrey, and in an instant they were on their separate ways. Mr. Eckhart trudged after her, grumbling under his breath.

Martin made his way deeper and deeper into the woods, and after a good quarter hour of shouting at the top of his lungs for his missing pet, his voice was getting hoarse. By the time he arrived at Winoka Lake, both his energy and his spirits were sagging.

He plopped down on his usual thinking rock. *How could this happen? How does a seven-foot-tall dinosaur just vanish? I should have known that latch wouldn't hold him. Where would he go? Doesn't he miss us? What if somebody else finds him? Or a hunter shoots him or something?!*

Not liking where this train of thought was going, Martin stood up and drew a deep breath for one big call across the lake.

*"Ruuuuuuu—"*

Hearing a rustling sound behind him, he cut off in midcall. His heart leaped as he spun around to see . . .

The absolute last person in the world he wanted to run into at this or any other moment: Donald Grimes.

"Heeeyy! Small world, huh, Tinky?"

By pure bad luck, Donald had chosen this time and this spot to do a bit of after-school fishing. He stood there, pole in one fist and tackle box in the other, grinning at Martin like an evil Cheshire cat.

Martin's face went blank, and their gazes locked for a long moment. Then—*voom!* He took off at maximum speed. Donald dropped his gear and streaked after him.

"Ohhhh, no. You're not getting away this time, you little slug!"

They flew through the woods, blasting through brush, vaulting over rocks and logs, skipping across a stream. Martin pumped his legs as fast as they would move, and actually managed to stay a comfortable distance ahead of Donald.

But his run of bad luck was not over. Just when he thought he might actually get away, he tripped on an exposed root and went sprawling to the ground. It was a muddy spot, and he couldn't get up fast enough to stop Donald from crashing on top of him like a TV wrestler.

"So, Tinkerbell. Try to make me look bad in front of *everybody,* huh?" He sat heavily on Martin's back, twisting his arm behind him.

"Ow! Grimes!"

"You know what happens to little guys with big yaps? They get their mouths washed out with mud. How would you like that, huh?"

"Leave me alone!" Martin rasped.

Donald scooped up a big handful of mud and got set to deliver it. "Snitchety snatch, down the hatch!"

Then, just as he was about to shove it in Martin's face . . .

*ROWWWRRR!*

Donald twisted around to see a twelve-foot-long, seven-foot-high tyrannosaur with rows of razor-sharp teeth and a look in its eye that was—well, not the look you want to see when you meet up with a seven-foot-tall tyrannosaur.

Donald, of course, had never seen anything quite like it before, and did exactly what his instincts dictated: he screamed like a banshee.

*"AAAAAAAAAAGGHHHH!"*

"Rufus!" Martin shouted.

*ROWWWWRRR!* Rufus replied, and immediately charged. Donald sprang off Martin and tried to scamper away, but Rufus cut him off and snapped at him angrily, barely missing his left foot.

"Rufus! No!" Martin hollered.

*"AAAAAAAAAAAGGHHHH!"* Donald screamed over and over as Rufus kept lunging and snapping at him. It was only by sheer luck that he didn't lose an arm—or worse.

Martin wrapped himself around Rufus's leg, trying to stop the onslaught. "No, don't hurt him! We were just playing. Stop! Rufus, no biting people!"

The extra weight slowed Rufus down just enough to give Donald a fighting chance.

"You're crazy, Tinker!" Donald gasped as he ducked and dodged more nimbly than he thought he knew how. "I quit! I promise I'll never bug you again!"

Rufus let out one more giant *ROWWWWRRR!* and took another snap at Donald, who finally spotted an escape route and rocketed off into the forest.

"Help! It's gonna eat me! I'm dying! Help, somebody, please! *He-e-e-e-elp . . .*"

His screams gradually faded as he disappeared into the woods. Martin knew this would lead to trouble, but for now he was glad the worst seemed to be over.

With his prey out of sight and, it would seem, out of mind, Rufus gradually calmed down, and Martin let go of his leg.

"Where have you been?" he scolded. "I was worried sick."

Rufus nuzzled him in the small of his back.

"Well, I found you, I guess that's the main thing. C'mon, we've got stuff to do."

He started on his way, but soon realized there were no footsteps behind him. He turned and saw Rufus standing there, sniffing at a low-hanging branch. He didn't seem in any particular hurry to go anywhere.

"Come *on,*" Martin insisted.

Rufus slowly, lazily fell into step behind him.


There was a big round rock, a good eight feet high and noticeably whiter than the other rocks nearby, that people used as a landmark to orient themselves in the woods. As Martin spotted it up ahead, he could see that Audrey and Mr. Eckhart were there waiting. It had been a half hour since he had split up with them, and they were both looking pretty nervous.

"Can't believe I'm letting a couple of seventh graders take me on some lame-brained unicorn hunt," Mr. Eckhart groused, pacing impatiently.

He wasn't paying attention as Martin appeared out of the brush, with Rufus trailing close behind. As the teacher bent over to tie a loose shoelace, his glasses fell off and he had to feel around on the ground for them.

"You found him!" Audrey shouted.

"This is Rufus, Mr. Eckhart," said Martin.

"Hmm, what?" he replied as he returned his glasses to their rightful place on his nose. Then, as the world came back into focus, he suddenly jumped a good three feet in the air. "What in the holy—"

With surprising athletic skill, he clambered on top of the white rock in about two seconds flat. "You weren't kidding!"

Alarmed by the sight of yet another strange human, Rufus growled and crouched down like a startled jungle cat.

"Relax, Rufus," Martin said. "He's a friend."

"You've got a bloody dinosaur!" Mr. Eckhart croaked from atop the rock.

"I told you we did," said Martin.

"Audrey, look out! Martin, watch your—get the— put the—"

"He's not dangerous, Mr. Eckhart," Audrey said calmly. "You don't have to stay up there."

*"What?"*

"Please, we need your help," said Martin. "Donald Grimes saw him and now everybody's gonna know."

Audrey's eyes widened. "Donald *saw* him?"

"He needs a real home. You're the only one we trust."

Mr. Eckhart was still too thunderstruck to register much of what Martin was saying. He squeezed his eyes shut and mumbled to himself. "Okay, this is not happening. It's three a.m., I'm sound asleep in my bed . . ."

"We need to get him back to the barn," said Audrey. "Please come back with us, Mr. Eckhart."

"I believe I'll stay right here, Audrey, if it's all the same to you."

Martin and Audrey looked at each other nervously. Maybe this whole thing hadn't been such a hot idea.

"Okay," Martin said, "stay here, and when he's in the barn we'll come back. Okay?"

"Uhhhhhhhh . . ."

Taking that as a yes, they headed off, with Rufus following.

Mr. Eckhart stayed put on the rock as they moved briskly down the footpath. Martin hoped that Mr. Eckhart would come down and follow once they got a safe distance ahead, and when he turned around to look, that was exactly what happened.

When Martin and Audrey arrived back at the barn, the big doors were still wide open, just as they had left them.

"C'mon, boy. Inside," Martin said as he stepped aside to let Rufus pass.

Rufus, though, had other ideas. He huffed and paced back and forth, ready to take off back into the woods.

"He doesn't want to go in," Audrey said ominously.

Martin tried to sound firm as he faced Rufus. "You can't stay out here. You have to go in now."

"Oh, wow . . . he's not gonna go in . . ."

Determined to prove her wrong, Martin snapped loudly, "Rufus! *In!* Now!"

His sudden burst of authority was enough to get Rufus's attention, and he slowly trudged through the opening into his unhappy cage. As Audrey closed the doors behind him, Martin went over and grabbed some cinder blocks from a nearby pile and stacked them in front of the doors so (he hoped) Rufus couldn't push them open again from inside.

Audrey pitched in. When they had laid down about a dozen blocks, Martin tugged hard on the doors; they didn't budge. "This should do it."

"You can come out now," Audrey called, and Mr. Eckhart, who had been hiding behind a tree at the edge of the woods, stepped forward.

"Okay, Peter," he said to himself as he approached stiffly. "You can wake up any old time now. Any . . . old . . . time."

"What should we do?" Audrey asked.

"Do? . . . Oh. Do. Um . . . okay. First, everybody just stay calm, and don't panic. What am I talking about? *I'm* panicking." He tried to peek through the crack between the barn doors. "Lord almighty! This is the . . . the greatest find in the *history* of—"

"Please, we have to get him out of here!" Martin almost shouted. "People are gonna come!"

"Okay. All right. Just give me a second here." Mr. Eckhart paced around, one hand on his hip, the other rubbing the back of his neck, repeatedly blowing out big gusts of air. Finally, he stepped up to Audrey. "Okay! Here's the deal. Give me the pictures."

She pulled the folded-up photos from her back pocket and handed them to him.

"Okay," he said, still a bit breathlessly. "Now, uh . . . what?" Martin and Audrey resisted the urge to roll their eyes, and Mr. Eckhart seemed to pick up on their impatience. "Okay!" he said, decisively. "I'll run these over to the U and talk to some people. Assuming they don't lock me up in a rubber room, maybe I can arrange something. Think you can hold out here for a while?"

"I guess so," said Martin.

"Super. Super-duper."

Mr. Eckhart started on his way, then turned back to shake each of their hands. He seemed to want to say something, but no words came out. He looked like a little kid at Christmas.

Finally, he turned and hustled off across the yard, emitting an exhilarated little *whoop!* along the way.

Martin and Audrey just stood there, wondering what to do next. He was feeling a bit uneasy, but it was a relief that at least they'd taken a first step.

"I've gotta get home," Audrey said. "Jade's gonna have a fit."

"I'll walk you."

They barely said a word to each other on the way to her house. But Martin knew she was thinking the same thing he was: one way or the other, their world was about to change.

# THIRTEEN

**M**artin took his time on the way back to his house. He was afraid of what might be going on there now, or would be soon, and he didn't want to face it just yet. So he walked really slowly, took a detour on Craig Street, and stopped in Hauser Park to watch a line of ants snaking their way up a tree trunk.

Then he saw a police car drive by. He wasn't sure, but the driver looked a lot like Sheriff Grimes—and sitting next to him was a kid who looked a whole *heck* of a lot like Donald. And they were heading straight toward the Tinkers' house.

As though hurled out of a giant slingshot, Martin took off after them. He knew there wasn't much chance of catching up to them, and he had no idea what he would do if he did anyway, but he somehow knew he had to get home *fast*.

It was a good four blocks of running, and by the time he got near his house he was plenty winded. He could see the squad car parked on the street in front, and Sheriff Grimes was headed up the walk to the front door.

Martin felt like maybe he should yell or something to distract him, but right then his mom's car appeared from the other direction and pulled into the driveway. He stood and watched from a neighbor's yard, panting like an overheated St. Bernard, as she got out and headed toward the front steps. Sheriff Grimes greeted her there, and they exchanged a few words. Martin couldn't hear what they were saying, but even though the sheriff looked calm and friendly, Mrs. Tinker definitely seemed concerned by what he was telling her. Finally, she opened the door, and they went in the house.

Martin stood there for a few seconds, wondering what to do next. Then he noticed that the squad car seemed to be empty. He stepped over and peeked in the back window, then the front. Suddenly, Donald's head popped up from below.

"*Agh!*" they both shouted at the same time.

"What are you doing here?" Martin snapped. "What did you tell him?"

"What do you think? You're a crazy freak with a giant tricycle tops!"

"He's a tyrann— Never *mind* . . ."

His heart sinking fast, Martin looked over at the house. Through the window, he could see Sheriff Grimes trying to explain something to his mom, who was looking back at him as though he had just stepped out of a Martian landing craft. She gestured for him to wait there, and went out into the kitchen.

Martin knew where she was going: out to the barn to look for him.

"I'd run if I were you," Donald croaked. "You're in deep doo-doo now, Huckleberry." He slid back down out of view. Martin had no idea what he was hiding from, but right now he couldn't dwell on how much of an idiot Donald was.

He saw a pickup truck approaching, and recognized it right away. His dad! Martin ducked behind a tree and peeked around as the truck pulled in the driveway and parked behind his mom's car. Sheriff Grimes opened the front door of the house and called to Mr. Tinker as he got out and headed up the walk.

"Hey there, Gordo!"

"What's the rap, Frank? I paid my taxes." Unlike Mrs. Tinker, he didn't seem all that concerned to see the sheriff in his house.

"No big deal, my friend. Just checking something out here, eh?"

Once they had gone inside, Martin emerged from behind the tree. But he still had no plan. All the ideas that came into his head were bad ones. He looked over at the police car and saw the top half of

Donald's prickly head peeking nervously out the window toward the house.

Deciding he needed to act now and think it through later, Martin took off around the side of the house, heading straight for the backyard. Maybe, by some miracle, he could still get Rufus out of the barn cellar before they discovered him.

As he was about to pass by an open living room window, he heard his dad and the sheriff talking inside. Ducking down to stay out of view, he stopped to listen.

Mr. Tinker laughed. "You can't be serious."

"Yeah, yeah, you know how kids are," said Sheriff Grimes. "Probably just some goofball prank. I'm just doing my job, eh?"

"Marty's a bit of a square peg, I'll give you that. But that'd be way out in left field, even for him."

He laughed again, which might have bugged Martin at another time, but right now he barely gave it a thought. He continued along the side of the house to the gate leading into the backyard—and froze when he looked across to the far end of the yard and saw his mom coming out of the barn workshop, through the side door.

She didn't look especially rattled; obviously she hadn't ventured around to the far end and seen the cinder blocks piled in front of the lower-level doors. So, figuring there was still a shot at keeping her in the dark, he raced toward her.

"Mom! Hi!" he called in a chipper voice. "Looking for me?"

"Martin, what is going on with you and the Grimes boy?"

She didn't sound the least bit chipper.

"Grimes?"

"He told the sheriff you had—"

With his usual terrible timing, Rufus poked his head right up to a cellar window. Martin's mom caught a tiny glimpse as he dropped back out of view.

"What have you got down there?" She went over to the window and stooped down, trying to see inside. "Martin, are you keeping an animal in there?" Her face was practically right up against the glass.

"Animal? Well, um . . . well, if by 'animal' you mean, like—"

Suddenly, Rufus appeared again, right on the other side of the glass from Mrs. Tinker's face. A thick pink tongue shot out between two rows of glistening teeth and slapped right against the pane, just an inch and a half from her nose.

With a monstrous gasp, she launched herself backward, landing flat on her butt.

Martin sucked in a lungful of air, his hands flying to the top of his head. "Ohhhhhhh, wow . . ."

His mom scrambled back on all fours like a panicked crab, emitting terrified little grunts. She seemed to want to scream, but her vocal cords must have seized up like a twisted garden hose, because nothing came out.

With quick little hops from one foot to the other, Martin started talking, hoping for the best. "Okay, he's kinda big, he looks scary and all, but he's really just a big puppy dog, y'know, this big, nice . . . nice, um . . . Mom? . . . Mom, wait!"

She had managed to find her feet and was running toward the house.

Martin looked over at the cellar window. "Rufus!" he growled through gritted teeth.

With nothing to guide him now but desperation, he ran around the corner to the back of the barn, slipping and sliding down the slope to the lower-level doors, and yanked away a cinder block. Maybe they could just make a break for it into the woods. But before he could pick up a second block, he heard the agitated voices of his dad, his mom, and the sheriff approaching fast from the house.

Ditching the quick-escape plan, Martin clambered back up the slope and raced around to the side door leading into his lab. As he rushed in and sprinted across the barn floor toward the trapdoor, he could hear the three of them arriving outside.

"Annie, *what* is going *on*?" said the sheriff.

"In there!" she rasped. "In there in there!"

*"What!"* said Mr. Tinker.

Martin threw open the trapdoor and dropped down to the cellar floor in three quick bounds, skipping over most of the steps. He spotted Rufus in a corner and rushed over, throwing his arms protectively around as much of the big guy as he could hold.

Just above them, Sheriff Grimes's face appeared in

a recessed window. He squinted. "What am I looking for?"

"Just look!" Mrs. Tinker squawked from behind him.

Rufus tensed up, and Martin held on tight, whispering urgently but reassuringly.

"We're gonna keep calm now, okay? It might get a little crazy, but we'll make it through if you just stay cool, all right? You can do that, *right*?"

"Ah geez, who put these . . ." It was his dad's voice, and it sounded somehow closer than the others. Martin froze, listening, trying to figure out what was going on out there.

It was strangely silent—all he could hear was the deep huffing of Rufus's breath. Then there was a faint *thunk* outside. Then came another, then another. The cinder blocks! His dad was tossing them away from the lower doors.

Martin jumped up.

His mom had apparently heard the same sound. "Oh, no. . . . Oh, no!" he heard her yell, running around from the side to the back of the barn. "No, Gordy! Don't open it!"

"Huh?"

A crack of light appeared between the doors, and in a flash, Rufus bounded across the room.

"Rufus, no!" Martin exclaimed in a whisper-shout.

*Bam!* The burly dino crashed into the doors, knocking them partway open.

"Jumping catfish!" Sheriff Grimes blurted out, and

through the narrow opening Martin could see his parents and the sheriff leap back from the doors like startled house cats. Mrs. Tinker let out a terrified howl and ran in the other direction.

"What in the bloody blazes is *that*?" Martin's dad shouted as Rufus kept banging against the doors, trying to bull his way through the crack, teeth-first.

There were just a few cinder blocks left at the base of the doors keeping him from pushing all the way through to freedom. But they were inching forward under his repeated charges. *Bam! . . . Bam!*

Martin leaped over and wrapped himself around Rufus's tail, trying to pull him back. But Rufus was too big, too strong, and too determined to get out to pay any attention to him at all.

The doors kept inching open. Martin could see his dad through the crack, standing there with an otherworldly expression on his face, while his mom watched from way back, her eyes like full moons. "Stay back, Ann," he said urgently. "Go in the house."

"Right, let's go," she said, edging away. "Gordy, Frank, come on!"

The two men just stood there, frozen, like they had no clue which way to go.

Then, suddenly, Mr. Tinker lowered his shoulder and hurled himself right at the double doors. *Wham!* He pushed against Rufus with everything he had, trying to get the door shut again.

The shock of being abruptly knocked back set something off in Rufus, and he pushed back angrily, teeth snapping and claws slashing through the opening, growling like a junkyard Rottweiler.

Mrs. Tinker was aghast. "Gordy, no! Just run!"

"You gonna help me out here, Frank?" Mr. Tinker barked at the sheriff, who snapped out of his stupor and jumped in to help. The two of them pushed as hard as they could, while doing their best to avoid those flying claws and teeth.

In the scuffle, Rufus's tail jerked hard and Martin got tossed into a pile of cardboard boxes. As he watched the struggle, he realized he hadn't ever seen his big pet quite so riled up, and for the first time he wondered if maybe there was something more to Rufus—something more dangerous—than he'd realized before. He had never felt so helpless in his life.

Finally, Mr. Tinker and the sheriff succeeded in getting Rufus back in and shutting the doors. Rufus kept growling and banging, but Martin could hear the cinder blocks getting stacked quickly back in place until the barrier was secure again.

Martin clambered out of the boxes and tried to grab hold of Rufus. "Shhhhh! Easy! Easy!" But Rufus was still all worked up, and in no mood to be comforted. Martin rushed over and put his ear up against the double doors.

He could hear his dad and the sheriff trying to catch their breath.

"Gordon," Sheriff Grimes said matter-of-factly, "if I was actually awake just now, and not in the middle of some whacked-out dream, I would say you've got a dinosaur in your barn."

"Don't be dense, Frank. Dinosaurs are extinct."

"Yeah? Then what would *you* call that thing?"

There was an excruciating silence. Martin bit down hard, fearing the worst was about to come. Then he heard his dad walking away, back toward the house.

"Where are you going?" said Mrs. Tinker.

"My rifle."

Martin gasped and went stiff as a ramrod.

"Forget that, Gordy," said the sheriff. "I'll take him out right now, eh?"

*"NOOOOO!"* Martin bellowed at the top of his lungs.

"Martin?" he could hear his mom exclaim.

"Holy geez, is he inside there?" his dad shouted.

*"NOOOO! NO GUNS!"* Martin rocketed across the cellar and shot up the stairs, flying through the trap-door.

As he raced over toward the lab area, his parents and Sheriff Grimes rushed in the side door.

"You can't shoot him!" Martin hollered. "He's not hurting anybody. *Please,* no guns, no shooting!"

His mom was slack-jawed. "You were *down there* with that thing?"

"Martin, what the bloody blazes is going on here?" his dad snapped.

"You got him all worked up," Martin said loudly. "He's not vicious or anything, but you have to—you can't just—"

"Wait a minute, wait a minute. You *knew* that thing was down there?"

"Yeah. I mean . . . well, yeah. But—"

"For how long?"

"If everybody could just, you know, like, calm down—"

"*How long,* Martin?"

Now, with his dad scowling and everybody's eyes focused on him like lasers, Martin was starting to feel a bit daunted.

"Four and a half months." He took a hard swallow and let out a puff of air. "I found him. I fed him, and raised him. He thinks I'm his mom."

The silence was deafening. Everybody gaped at him as though he had just dropped a boulder on a priceless Ming vase.

"Oh, lord," Mrs. Tinker droned, a vaguely astonished look of recognition on her face. "The deformed lizard . . ."

Martin gave a pained little grin and a tiny shrug.

"What *is* that thing, son?" Sheriff Grimes asked.

Martin hesitated. "It's um . . . it's a, um . . ." He cleared his throat and faked a cough, covering his mouth. "T. rex."

"A what?" his dad said.

"T. rex."

Now the silence was even heavier—until it was broken by two loud *roars* from below.

Mrs. Tinker let out a faint moan, and her knees

buckled. The sheriff grabbed her arm and steadied her.

"But it's all okay now," Martin said, with new purpose. "I told Mr. Eckhart, and he went over to the U, and they're gonna, they're gonna—"

"Who's Mr. Eckhart?" Mr. Tinker said sharply.

"My science teacher. He said he can help. He's gonna find a good place for him"—Rufus *roared* again, and Martin had to talk loudly to be heard over the din— "and so that'll work out really well because that way nobody—"

"All right, stop. Stop! Don't talk," his dad interjected. "I need to think." He started pacing, a look of intense concentration on his face.

"Look," Mrs. Tinker said, "let's all just go in the house for now, okay? We can call the police, and then things can—"

"I'm already here, Ann," said Sheriff Grimes, with barely concealed annoyance.

"Right, of course. Sorry."

"Holy geez," said Mr. Tinker, gaping down through the trapdoor. "Will you just *look* at that thing."

Rufus let out another *roar*.

"Can't we just leave him alone?" Martin implored. "He's not used to having all these people around."

"I swear I thought I'd seen just about everything," his dad muttered as he watched the scaly creature bobbing around below him.

"Okay, why don't you all just stay put for now," said

the sheriff. "I've got a tranquilizing rifle back at the station, I'll just go and—"

"No!" Martin shouted. "You can't shoot him!"

"Not with bullets, son. Just something to put him to sleep."

As he headed for the door, Martin raced after him. "He doesn't need to sleep! You just got him all excited. You don't have to shoot him!"

His mom grabbed him by the arm. "All right, Martin, enough."

"Why does he have to shoot him? He's not hurting anybody. I can handle him! Why can't we just wait until—"

"Martin, you need to be quiet!" his dad barked. "You go on up to the house. Go to your room and stay there. We'll deal with you later. Your mother and I need to talk."

Martin looked up at his mom, a look of desperation on his face. She let go of his arm, but her eyes had the same chilly glare as his dad's. "Go on."

And so, his heart leaden, Martin trudged out of the barn, across the yard, into the house, and up the stairs to his room. He could only imagine what they were talking about down there in the barn, but he tried hard not to think about it. Because the one thing he knew for sure was that the big loser in the deal was going to be Rufus.

# FOURTEEN

**F**or twenty minutes Martin paced in his room. It seemed like he might wear a hole in his shoes, but he didn't care. His mind kept getting yanked back to what his parents were probably talking about down there. Sell Rufus to some circus? Bring in a bunch of heartless researchers to dissect him like a frog? Shoot him in cold blood and mount his head on the wall like a moose? The possibilities were bad, worse, and unthinkable.

Martin kept stopping at the window to look out across the yard to the barn. Rufus wasn't roaring anymore, and the long silence was starting to drive Martin nuts. Finally, he saw his parents come out of the lab and head back to the house. They seemed calmer than before, but then the worst possible thing happened: Martin heard a car door slam out front, and moments later Sheriff Grimes was in the house again—and there was somebody with him. Martin quietly opened the bedroom door and tiptoed out onto the landing, from where he could see a sliver of the living room as they all gathered there. There was something long and dark in the sheriff's hand, and the sight of it made Martin's blood run cold. He'd never seen a tranquilizing rifle before, and he didn't like the looks of this one, not one bit.

The first one to talk was the man who came in with Sheriff Grimes, and Martin recognized the loud, boisterous voice immediately: Ben Fairfield.

"Hey there, Gordo! Annie. I understand there's something to see in your barn."

"You heard that, huh?" Mr. Tinker said coolly.

"Yeah, how 'bout that," the sheriff chirped. "Right when I pull up, who's driving by but Ben?"

"Oh, you know how it goes," said Mr. Fairfield. "Wherever Frank is, that's where there's trouble. Ha ha haaa! So what do you think? Can we have a look?"

His parents mumbled something Martin couldn't make out; then the whole group headed toward the kitchen. Martin scurried back to the bedroom window and watched as they filed out into the backyard and made their way to the barn, gathering around a lower-level window.

Mr. Fairfield stooped down to look inside, and Martin could tell he saw Rufus down there, because he quickly jumped to his feet and looked at the other three, bug-eyed. A big grin spread across his face, and he stooped down to the window again. He watched Rufus for a bit; then, for some strange reason, he started laughing. He laughed harder, then leaned in close and made some weird barking noises, like he was trying to get a rise out of Rufus. Hooting like a chimpanzee, he tapped on the glass and waved his hands tauntingly.

Martin kicked the wall. This was just too much.

He bolted out of the room and raced down the stairs, through the kitchen, and out into the yard. He felt like marching right in there and giving them all a piece of his mind, but he thought better of it and ducked down behind the concrete birdbath in the center of the yard to watch and listen.

Mr. Fairfield wasn't laughing or waving his hands anymore, but he was still stooped down at the barn window, watching Rufus with an oversize smirk frozen on his face like a mask. Martin could see Rufus's head zipping back and forth as he paced restlessly inside.

"My oh my oh my," Mr. Fairfield said, dragging out each syllable for maximum drama. "If that doesn't top it all."

"You might want to stay back, Ben," said Mrs. Tinker. "We don't want to get him too riled up."

"My oh my oh my," Mr. Fairfield said again, still staring down at Rufus. "So where'd that thing come from, Gordy?"

"Martin came up with it."

"*Came up* with it?"

"Yeah, I dunno. He'll have to explain it."

"My oh my oh my," said Mr. Fairfield once more, in case anybody had missed it. Finally, he got up from the barn window and stepped over to Martin's parents. "So what are you gonna do with it?"

"That's, uh, to be determined," Mr. Tinker said.

"Well, you can't keep it here," said the sheriff. "You know that, right?"

"I know that, Frank," said Mr. Tinker curtly. "Maybe you've got some bright idea of what to do with it."

"Wait a minute, hold the phone," Mr. Fairfield chimed in. "I think I might be able to help out in that regard."

"How's that?" Martin's dad said.

"Let's try looking at this from a purely practical standpoint. What you've got down there is a tangible asset of some value."

Martin stiffened. He knew this was coming.

"What we've got is a dangerous wild animal in our barn," said Mrs. Tinker.

"Short-term problem." Mr. Fairfield was still grinning. "Look, I'll just cut right to it, okay? How much you want for it?"

Martin's jaw clenched. He almost pushed over the birdbath.

Mr. Tinker ran his fingers across his scalp. "I dunno, Ben. I was thinking maybe it . . . belongs in a science lab or something."

"Sure, sure, absolutely. I'm just saying there's no reason not to . . . maximize the short-term potential *first*. Then later *on* . . ."

Martin's mom and dad exchanged a look.

"I've got everything in place for it," Mr. Fairfield said. "I can make it worth everybody's while."

Martin's dad let out a long, drawn-out breath. "What've you got in mind?"

Martin had heard enough.

"He's not for sale!"

He sprang out from behind the birdbath and charged into the group, eyes ablaze, lips trembling. "*I* found his egg, and he belongs to *me*!"

"Whoa, slow down there, bud," his dad snapped. "You think that thing belongs to *you*?"

"I earned my own money and I fed him and I raised him!"

"Didn't I tell you to stay in your room? You need to get back up there right now."

"I won't let you sell him!"

"Nobody's decided anything. Now get on up there. Go on."

"If you sell my dinosaur, I'll—I'm gonna—I'm gonna—"

"*Martin*. Room. Now."

Martin just stood there, shaking with anger. He'd never talked to his dad like this before, and even though it was kind of scary, somehow it felt completely right. He could sense it was throwing his dad off a bit too.

But Mr. Tinker did not back down. He walked straight up to Martin and hovered over him menacingly.

Martin stared up at him, jaw jutting out, trying hard not to blink. Then he looked over at his mom, hoping that maybe she would speak up for him. But she just stood there, showing no hint of sympathy. He looked back at his dad and said what he knew he shouldn't.

"You're a jerk!"

As he spun around and bolted across the yard toward the house, his mom let out a gasp. "Martin!"

He could hear her following him but pretended he didn't as he ran inside and let the door slam behind him. He knew where he was supposed to be headed, but when he got to the base of the stairs his legs just kept on going. He shot straight through the living room and out the front door.

There was a big maple tree at the side of the front yard, and something told him that was where he was going, so he ran straight over to it and started climbing. Maybe if he could just get high enough, he could somehow leave behind all the rotten, stupid stuff taking place at ground level.

Unfortunately he wasn't much of a climber, and he was still struggling to pull himself onto a low branch when his mom caught up.

"Martin, you do not get to talk like that! What are you doing? Come down from there."

"Leave me alone." His hand got pricked by a sharp twig. "Ow!"

"You're going to hurt yourself. Martin, *stop.*"

He pulled himself up onto the limb and tried to stand up to reach the next one, but his foot slipped and he dropped to the ground in a heap.

"Oh! Good lord!" his mom exclaimed.

She ran over to check if he was okay. Martin sat up quickly, but when she stooped down next to him, he turned away.

"Leave me alone!"

"You need to stop. Just take a breath, will you?"

Martin stared off into the trees, eyes narrowed, chest heaving, lips contorted. They sat there for a good minute or so without speaking, which was just fine with him, since he was in no mood for a chat. But he could tell she was pretty wound up herself.

Finally, she stood up again and let him have it.

"Martin, are you out of your *mind*? You were keeping that thing down there the whole summer, after I *told* you to get rid of it? What were you thinking?"

"He's not a thing! He's my friend."

"Really? And what if me or your dad or somebody else had gone down there? How friendly would he have been then?"

"He wouldn't have hurt you."

"Right, and you're such an expert on wild animals that you know *exactly* what they'll do. And oh, by the way, an animal that nobody has seen before, *ever.*"

As far as Martin was concerned, this was all getting completely off the subject. "Dad's gonna sell him, right?" he blurted out as he suddenly spun around to face her. "Both of you. You'll sell him to Mr. Fairfield, and then they'll make him into a freak show, and he'll be miserable the rest of his life."

"We don't know that. It's all up in the air right now. Anyway, you had to know sooner or later *somebody*—"

"How can you take Dad's side? I thought you cared. He's a jerk!"

"Hey! You do not talk about your father that way!"

Martin drooped his head between his knees, forehead nearly to the ground. His mom paced around for a bit, letting out an occasional heavy breath. She stopped and studied him for a long time, and then, seeming much calmer, sat down next to him.

"You know, this may come as a shock to you . . . but your father loves you a lot more than you realize."

He gave a disdainful splutter.

"Hey, I would know, don't you think? Let me tell you something. Back in high school, when I first met your dad, I thought he was a jerk too. Just this arrogant jock with a swelled head from having so many girls at his feet. Then one day during a game, he was going for a ball and he accidentally ran over a boy on the sideline. Broke the kid's collarbone. But you know what, he didn't just walk away. He stayed with the boy until the ambulance got there, and he visited him in the hospital and really went out of his way to be nice to him for the rest of the year. That's when I knew there was a sweet guy inside the tough outer shell."

Martin lifted his head up just enough to deliver his

sarcastic retort. "Well, the shell must have hatched, because the sweet guy is gone."

With the beginnings of a smile, his mom reached over and rubbed his back. "He just wants to keep us all safe. So do I. You get that, don't you?"

Actually, Martin did kind of get that. What he didn't get was what anybody was going to do to keep *Rufus* safe.

"Come on," she said, standing up. "Just go on up for now, and we'll all get together later and talk about it. We'll figure it all out." She kept looking straight at him. "Okay, potato-puss?"

He threw her a sidelong sneer.

"Sorry," she said with a half smile. "I can't help myself."

Martin didn't smile, but he got up and trudged back into the house with her. He wanted to believe it would all work out. Maybe they really would listen to him, and maybe Rufus would get a decent deal out of it.

But when he got back up to his room and looked out the window, all his fears started bubbling up again. The three men were down there in the yard, talking. Sheriff Grimes had his stupid tranquilizing gun, and now Mr. Tinker had a long wooden stick and a big roll of telephone cord in his hands. Martin had seen that roll sitting in a corner of his barn lab, and now the stick and cord were obviously going to be put to some use he didn't even want to imagine.

Meanwhile, Mr. Fairfield was doing most of the talking, waving his hands around as he made his points. Martin tried to listen to what was being said. He couldn't make out much of it, but a few of Mr. Fairfield's louder phrases came through: "seven figures . . . cash cow . . . fifty-fifty partnership . . . absolute blockbuster . . ."

Martin's stomach gnarled up, and his heart began racing again. This was not how things were supposed to go.

He started pacing around once more, thinking, thinking, thinking. If only he could reach Mr. Eckhart. But how? He was probably just arriving at the U. Maybe Audrey would have an idea. Martin realized he'd left his phone on the kitchen counter. But his mom was in there, so he would have to sneak down and get it without her seeing.

He looked out the window and saw the sheriff open up his tranquilizing rifle and run a cleaning brush down the barrel. If anything was going to be done to help Rufus, it had to be *now*.

He cooked up a desperate plan. If he could get into the woods through the trailhead down at the end of his street, he might be able to circle around and slip into the backyard at the far end of the barn, and probably nobody would see him there. Then he could pull away the cinder blocks, free Rufus, and head off into the woods, just the two of them, and stay hidden out there until Mr. Eckhart got back. Or at least until he could think up a better plan.

Martin slipped quietly out of the bedroom and peeked down the stairs. Coast clear. He tiptoed down and spotted his mom in the kitchen, watching the others in the backyard through the window—probably as close as she wanted to get. He crept silently into the kitchen, grabbed his phone from the counter, and then slunk out into the hall, glided across the living room, and flew out the front door.

He could almost hear the precious seconds ticking away as he ran down the street. He knew he would need somebody to alert Mr. Eckhart where he was, so, without slowing down a bit, he switched on the phone and dialed Audrey's home number.

"Come on . . . come on, answer." Four rings. Five rings. Where was she? He'd just walked her home an hour ago! Six rings. Why couldn't she have her own cell phone? Flustered, he clicked off the phone and dropped it in his pocket.

Though it was only a quarter mile from there to the trailhead, by the time Martin got there he was pretty well spent. Still, he knew he couldn't let that slow him down, and he pushed on into the woods. As planned, he hooked straight back around toward the house—but, not knowing this particular set of trails very well, he made a couple of wrong turns and ended up at the white rock instead. Totally annoyed, he gave the rock a hard kick—which only made things worse, because now he had a bruised toe.

He knew the way back from there, but had already lost an extra ten minutes. So when he finally arrived at the far end of the yard, his whole body went limp when he saw that his dad and the others weren't there anymore—which could only mean they had already gone into the barn to do their dirty work.

Martin swallowed hard. He didn't know which was more alarming—what they might do to Rufus, or what he might do to them. Either way, he had a sickening feeling he was too late to do anything about it.

He raced over to the double doors and tried to peek in through the tiny slit between them. The view wasn't very good, but he could make out the tops of three men's heads behind a row of wooden crates. They were kneeling down, doggedly working on something on the ground in front of them. Martin couldn't tell who was who, but they sounded pretty tense as they worked.

"You got that one?"

"Yeah, it's good. Wait—"

"Whoa, whoa, whoa!"

"I got it, I got it."

"Easy does it. *Easy.*"

"Okay. I think we're there. All good."

They slowly stood up, all breathing hard but looking hugely relieved.

*"Wow,"* said Mr. Fairfield. "Not bad for three old guys, eh?"

"Speak for yourself, buddy," said the sheriff, and all three of them chuckled.

Something moved just a bit on the floor in front of their feet, and Martin knew right away what it was: the tip of Rufus's tail, sticking out from behind the crates. The worst had obviously already happened:

they had tranquilized him and tied him up with the phone cord.

Martin's heart was palpitating, his teeth grinding. He wanted to scream out, but there was a giant lump in his throat blocking his voice box.

"Whoo!" Sheriff Grimes sighed. "For a minute there I thought my head was gonna get bit off."

"Ha ha!" Mr. Fairfield cackled. "When he came at us like that, I thought we were *all* done for."

"Good thing you didn't miss," said Mr. Tinker.

Hearing them joke about it did nothing at all to loosen the knot in Martin's gut. He just wanted to smash the doors in, tear those cords off Rufus, and fly him off to another planet where the people weren't so heartless.

"So what now?" Mr. Tinker said.

"We wrap him up in that tarp over there," said Ben Fairfield, pointing to a big piece of canvas in a corner, "and load him up in your truck and take him to the Trout Palace."

"You got a place to put him there?" the sheriff asked.

"For now we can just lock him up in the mainte-nance shed. That should work for a week or two."

"Is that gonna be secure?" said Martin's dad.

"Sure, sure. I'll see to it nobody goes near there. You told your kid to keep his mouth shut, right?"

Martin was only a tiny bit relieved that Mr. Fair-field had addressed that one to Sheriff Grimes, not his dad.

"Oh, yeah. No problem with Donnie," the sheriff said.

"After we close next week, we'll make a nice big holding area for him, get him good and fattened up over the winter. By next spring, we should be good to go. Gordy, why don't you and Ann come over there first thing in the morning and we'll talk some business."

Suddenly, there was a grunt from behind the crates, and Rufus's tail swung weakly toward their feet. They all jumped back, and Mr. Fairfield quickly grabbed the stick out of Mr. Tinker's hand and took a swing at the body on the floor in front of them. The *thump* sound of wood on rib cage pierced Martin's heart like an ice pick.

"No!" Fairfield barked. "Down!"

He took another whack. Martin nearly jumped out of his shoes.

"Ben, easy," Martin's dad implored. "He's not going anywhere."

"Hey, a dangerous animal like that, you've got to show him who's boss. Who's up, who's down, that's all they understand."

When he reached back to take a third whack, Martin had seen and heard enough. He suddenly pounded his hands on the wooden doors with everything he had. *Bam! Bam! Bam! Bam! Bam!*

"What in creation—?" said Sheriff Grimes.

*Bam bam bam bam!*

"Who's out there?" Mr. Tinker called.

"You can't have him!" Martin cried out, fighting against tears that threatened to choke him. "He's my friend and I won't let him go!" *Bam bam bam!*

"Criminy, he's down here *again*?" Mr. Tinker muttered, heading quickly for the cellar stairs.

Martin knew his dad would be out there in a flash; rather than face him, he wheeled around and took off at full speed into the woods.

He ran and ran, not even noticing that it was starting to get dark out there. As far as he was concerned, if he got lost or fell and broke his leg or got eaten by some deadly night creature, that was just fine with him.

But he didn't get lost or break a bone or get eaten; within a few minutes he found himself at a very familiar spot: the shore of Winoka Lake. He plopped down on his thinking rock and buried his head in his hands, rubbing his temples as though trying to erase all the awful sights and sounds he'd absorbed that day.

He saw a drop of water hit the ground below him, leaving an amoeba-shaped blob of mud on the smooth, gray dirt. A second drop fell, and he realized it wasn't raindrops, but his own tears.

He took a long, deep gulp of air and lifted his head to gaze out across the surface of the lake, shimmering in the approaching dusk. He stared hard at the thousands of spots of light as they ignited and then quickly vanished, hoping maybe he could vanish along with them, and then reappear sometime in the far future when all this stuff would be just a vague memory.

A crackling sound jarred him out of his sullen daydream, and he glanced back to see his dad approaching. He hadn't expected to be discovered quite so quickly. Not wanting to provide even the slightest reminder of the Orville-the-hamster situation, he quickly brushed the salt water off his cheeks and fixed a steely gaze on the horizon.

Mr. Tinker didn't yell, like Martin expected he would; instead, he slowly wandered up and stopped a few feet behind him.

"Hey," he said calmly.

Martin pretended not to hear; he just kept staring out over the lake. His dad sauntered over and sat down on another rock nearby.

"Look, uh . . . I know you're not on board with this. I get that. You got attached. But don't forget, it was you that broke the rules. We told you, no pets. *Especially* a beast like that thing."

Trying to hold his tongue, Martin exhaled tightly.

"But you know what, we don't have to dwell on that. What you obviously haven't thought about is the good that's gonna come out of this. Things'll be a little easier for us all for a change. Plus, you'll probably be the most popular kid in school. I'd say it's a pretty good deal."

Martin whirled around and faced him. "How could you sell him? To jerky Ben Fairfield, of all people! Now he's just gonna be some stupid circus act!"

"What did you think was going to happen, Martin?! Did you think you were just gonna keep that thing down there forever? What kind of parents would that make us, when it got twelve feet tall and decided to make a lunch out of you?"

"He would never do that!"

"You don't know that, and you *know* you don't!"

Martin jumped to his feet, picked up a stick, and threw it out into the lake as far as he could.

As he paced around, his dad watched him with a taut frown. "Tell you what," he said. "We'll let you get a pet. A dog or something. You like dogs, right?"

Martin gave a dismissive snort. Now it was his dad who jumped to his feet.

"For crying out loud, Martin, you are almost twelve years old! When are you gonna learn how to take things like a man?"

"I'm not a man!" Martin shot back, facing him square-on. "And if it means being greedy and heartless like you, I'd rather not be one!"

"Hey!" his dad barked, pointing a stiff finger straight at his nose. Martin knew he'd crossed the line with that one, and figured this would be the start of an all-out tongue-lashing. But instead Mr. Tinker slowly lowered his finger, looked away, and softened his tone.

"Look, I'll do everything I can to see he's treated well. That's all I can promise you. We can sit down later and hash it out. Right now we need to get back. It's getting dark out here. C'mon."

Martin picked up a stone and tried to skip it across the water, but it just plopped straight in.

"Let's go, pal," his dad said.

Martin shuffled around for a few more seconds. Then, without saying a word, he turned around and sprinted back down the path—by himself, not with his dad.

He ran all the way back, went straight into the house, breezed past his mom, and stomped up the stairs to his room.

Martin didn't want to watch as Mr. Tinker backed his truck into the yard, and then he and the sheriff and Mr. Fairfield headed around to the far end of the barn. Minutes later they emerged pushing a large wheelbarrow with Rufus, now limp and rolled up in a tarp, draped across it. With great effort, they wheeled their bulky cargo up the slope and, with a lot of grunting and straining, managed to load it into the truck bed.

As much as Martin hated watching this, he couldn't *not* look either, and he stood there in the bedroom window, breathing heavily, as the scene unfolded below. What was even worse was what happened after they finished the deed: Mr. Fairfield pulled something out of his pocket, scribbled something down, tore off a small, rectangular sheet of paper, and handed it to Martin's dad—a check, sealing the deal.

Martin slammed the window shut, flopped back on

the bed, and turned up the clock radio really loud with rap music. He stayed there for a long time, hoping his mind would drift to other things. But he just couldn't shake the thought of everything that had happened—and he feared that the worst was yet to come.

The rest of the evening came and went, and Martin barely moved, except to go over and sit down next to the window to stare out at the full September moon. The big talk his parents promised never happened, but that was fine with him; right now he just wanted to be left alone. He refused even to go downstairs for dinner. He decided he would simply stay in that room for the rest of his miserable life, until he shriveled up and turned into a dusty skeleton. They'd have to haul what was left of him out of there in a Hefty bag. Yes, he'd show them, all right.

But then his mind went back to poor Rufus. He *couldn't* just sit back and do nothing while they treated him like some giant carnival freak. But what could an eleven-year-old kid possibly do?

There *had* to be *something*.

# FIFTEEN

*Even in its best days, the Trout Palace had never seen crowds like this. A huge circus tent had been put up on the grounds, and people were jammed in by the thousands. They were all buzzing excitedly and jostling for the best view of the big stage set up at one end of the tent.*

*Ben Fairfield, dressed in a snappy tuxedo, strutted out from behind the curtain to the center of the stage, a bright spotlight following him. He stepped up to a microphone and waited patiently as the hubbub turned to dead silence.*

*"Folks, you've heard about it," he said dramatically. "You've read about it, and now you've come from all over the world to see it for yourselves. So I'm not going to make you wait for it one moment longer.*

Ladies and gentlemen, I give you . . . Tyrannosaurus rex!"

A blast of loud music suddenly struck up over the PA system, and slowly the curtain rose to reveal a huge prehistoric beast, shackled at the neck and feet while chained to a thick metal post. Rufus was now a fully grown tyrannosaur, almost twenty feet tall, and the sight of him drew a huge gasp from the crowd. Their speechless amazement gave way to a chorus of astonished murmurings. Then, when the sight of this fearsome creature had fully registered in their brains, a wave of thunderous applause swept across the sea of people like a tidal wave.

But Rufus was not looking at all fierce or vicious. He twitched and squirmed, blinded by the bright lights and weighed down by the chains. Even worse, every time he tried to pull free, one of three men dressed all in black would jolt him with a long electric cattle prod to keep him in line.

People clapped and whistled. Cameras flashed like a lightning storm. Children pointed in amazement. Babies cried. The music continued to throb, shaking the whole tent.

Way in the back, Martin was trying to push through the crowd toward the stage. But he could hardly move, everybody was packed in so tight. He twisted and squeezed and shoved, trying desperately to get to the stage so he could some way, somehow put an end to the outrageous spectacle.

He could see, just offstage, his parents and Mr.

*Fairfield exchanging delighted smiles, beaming at the sensation they'd created.*

*For Rufus, it was all too much. The chains, the prods, the throngs, the noise . . . it brought him right to the point of panic. Agonized, he reared back and let loose with a long, thunderous ROAR—and the sound triggered something in Martin and he threw his own head back and let out a shrill, deeply pained* "NOOOOOOOOO!"

Martin bolted upright in his bed. Darkness engulfed him, and his eyes darted around in confusion. He was panting hard; sweat covered his body. Then, as his head cleared, he felt his muscles gradually loosen a bit. Never had he been so relieved to awaken from a dream.

But his relief didn't last long. He jumped out of bed and paced furiously back and forth. To just sit and do nothing while they turned Rufus into a cheesy circus act . . . well, it simply was not an option.

He went to the window and gazed out at the moon, his mind racing. His thoughts quickly started coming together. Fact one: Rufus was imprisoned at the Trout Palace. He would have to be freed. Fact two: Ben Fairfield did not have Rufus's best interests at heart. Fact three: Mr. Eckhart was still the only hope. Somehow, he would have to be found.

"Don't worry, Rufus," he said to the black sky, with a new, steely resolve. "I'll take care of you."

He looked over at the dimly lit clock radio next to his bed: 4:45 a.m.

With fierce determination, he threw on some clothes in record time, raced downstairs very quietly, slipped out the side door, and jumped on his bike. He pedaled off into the darkness at top speed, which was probably not the smartest thing to do, since his bike had no light. He hit a couple of bumps and nearly wiped out two different times, but somehow managed to keep it together.

As he rode, a plan started taking shape in his head. He knew where Mr. Fairfield kept the keys in his office, and with luck, he could sneak in there and get them. Then, while Audrey created a distraction for the night guards, he would open up the maintenance shed and free Rufus. Then all three of them would slip out the gate in the chain-link fence at the back of the Trout Palace grounds. From there they could escape into the woods and make their way to Mr. Eckhart's house.

Martin knew if he thought about it too much, he would realize what an outlandish plan it was, and he might lose his enthusiasm. So for now, he didn't think any more about the details.

In just minutes, he made it all the way to the Blanchards' house.

Martin rode into the front yard, vaulted off his bike like a gymnast dismounting a pommel horse, and ran around the side of the house to where he knew Audrey's room was. He waded through some low bushes to get to the window, then tapped quietly on the glass. No response. He tapped louder, and finally a surprised and groggy-eyed Audrey opened the window.

"What are you doing?!" she rasped.

"We have to save Rufus. They took him to the Trout Palace and they're gonna make him into a freak show."

"Ai-yai-yai . . ."


From behind an evergreen bush on a wooded ridge just beyond the back fence of the Trout Palace grounds, Audrey and Martin scoped out the scene. From there they had a pretty good view of the whole place. It was strange to him how a place that was so bright and loud and full of life during the day could be so dark and eerily quiet at night.

He had told Audrey his plan, and to his surprise, she hadn't asked a lot of annoying questions or tried to point out all the flaws. He was glad to know she was as committed to freeing Rufus as he was.

"So, which building?" she asked in a hushed voice.

He pointed to a dull gray structure, about the size of a two-car garage, that was right next to the fence, away from the main building. It was used to store tools, lawn equipment, restaurant supplies, and whatever else might need a home from time to time. At the moment, it was also home to a seven-foot-tall tyrannosaur. At least, that was what Martin assumed from having overheard Mr. Fairfield talking to his dad.

"So you can get the key for that, right?" Audrey said. She was referring to the roll-up gate that filled the front wall of the storage shed, secured by what looked like a giant padlock.

"Yeah . . . but I'm kinda more worried about *him*."

Yes, "him" was going to be a problem. The night guard, a pudgy, unshaven guy named Ollie Thwait, was sitting right next to the shed gate underneath a lonely floodlight mounted on the corner of the building, deeply absorbed in some phone app game.

"He doesn't usually stay in one spot like that. They must've told him to stay there."

"Uch. . . . So what do we do?"

"We need to get him away from there."

"Okay. . . . How?"

Martin chewed on his lower lip for a moment, then stood up and started tiptoeing down the ridge. He motioned to Audrey, and she followed.

They worked their way along the outside of the chain-link fence, well beyond the storage shed, until they reached a gravel driveway that led to a wheeled gate that rolled open to allow service vehicles in and out. It was locked and chained, but that didn't slow Martin down; he dropped to the ground and slithered through the narrow opening under the gate next to the wheels.

As he emerged on the other side, Audrey looked at him with a blank expression.

"You're as skinny as me," he half whispered. "Come on."

She gave a tiny shrug, then dropped down and slipped underneath the gate as easily as Martin had.

They followed the narrow pathway between the fence and the main building until they reached a small window, which Martin pushed open.

Climbing through the window, they found themselves in the kitchen of the Heart o' the Woods restaurant. As Audrey followed Martin into the dining area, she couldn't help slowing down to check out the odd sight of a line of fishing poles leaning against the wall. He motioned to her to hurry up, and they made their way into the eerily dark and deserted main hall.

"I can't see," she whispered.

"Just follow me."

He led her to a secluded corner and flipped on a few light switches; enough fixtures went on for them to see their way around a bit better.

"Just go to all those booths and look for the 'on' switch," Martin said. "But don't flip 'em yet. I'll be right back."

"Okay," she said nervously as he slipped away. "Wait a minute, how do I— Martin?" Too late. He was well on his way.

He dashed over into a short hallway and stepped inside Mr. Fairfield's office. Having done some cleaning in there many times before, he knew exactly where to go: a key box on the wall just next to the door.

He threw open the box and gaped at the keys hanging on hooks. He didn't remember there being quite so many—there were at least fifteen or twenty. Not knowing which one was which, he just grabbed the whole bunch and stuffed them in his pockets.

As he ran back out into the main hall, keys jangling, he spotted Audrey across the way, examining the U-Bag-Em game. He trotted over and pointed out the big red Start button.

"This one."

"Ah. Right. You got the keys?"

"Yeah. So just start with this one and do the same thing on all these."

"Okay . . ."

She looked a little unsure, so he led her over to a ring-toss booth next to a small alcove and showed her the button.

"See? Easy."

"Okay. Got it."

"When I go, count to a hundred, then just start flipping as many as you can. But do it fast, and then get out."

She threw him a wry look. "Really? I was hoping to get caught."

Suddenly, there was a high-pitched *shriek,* and they nearly jumped out of their shoes. Rigid and wide-eyed, they looked into the alcove—and saw that they had just awakened the furry inhabitants of the musk-rat cages. Breathing easier, they shared an unsteady smile.

"Meet me back at the service gate," Martin said with back-to-business seriousness.

"Okay," Audrey said, and swallowed hard.

"See ya."

"One Mississippi, two Mississippi, three Mississippi . . ."

As he sprinted back over toward the restaurant, he couldn't shake the thought that he was in way over his head with this crazy scheme and they'd both end up in juvenile hall. But there was a battlefield general in his head, telling him to keep pushing, pushing, pushing the whole thing forward.

He raced through the dining area, scampered into the kitchen, and climbed back outside through the open window. As he ran along the fence back toward the storage shed, he had to grab onto his pants pockets tightly to keep the keys from making an unholy racket. He knew he must have looked pretty dorky running like that, but right now that was last on his list of concerns.

As he neared the storage shed, he slipped behind a propane tank and peeked out at Ollie, still parked in his chair right next to the rolling gate in the front of the shed. It was pretty clear that it was going to take a lot to move him out of there.

Martin stooped low behind the tank, trying to keep as quiet as possible. Two minutes went by, then three, then four. What was taking so long? Maybe Audrey couldn't find the switches. Or maybe she had, but it was too far away for Ollie to see or hear. Or maybe—Jasper!

He had completely forgotten about Jasper. He was the other night guard, and if he was anywhere near the Trout Palace building, Audrey could get caught, the whole plan would go down the drain, and the next stop for both of them would be the county lockup.

Martin's heart was beating a mile a minute. He gripped his key-laden pockets tightly with his sweating palms, his anxiety burning hotter and hotter. He felt like he might faint any second. Then . . .

Ollie quickly stood up and looked over toward the main building. He picked up a walkie-talkie and put it to his mouth.

"Jasper. . . . Jasper."

Martin held his breath as Ollie waited a moment, then pushed the Talk button again.

*"Jasper."*

After a long pause, a crackly voice came on. "What's up, Ollie?"

"Where are you?"

"I'm in the can. What do you want?"

"Did you just turn on some lights in the Palace?"

"I just finished telling you. I'm in the can."

"You need to get your butt in there right now. Somebody went in."

"Uhhhh, that's gonna be a negative."

"What do you mean, a negative?"

"I'm gonna be in here a while. I think I ate some bad cheese fries."

Ollie gave a muffled growl and looked for a moment like he might fling the walkie-talkie at the wall. Then he froze, hearing something. It was pretty faint, but

Martin and Ollie both recognized it right away—a deep voice delivering a familiar refrain:

*"Ho ho ho ho! Welcome to the Trout Palace! Thirty acres of pure Wisconsin fun . . ."*

Martin never thought he would be so happy to hear that ridiculous talking fish. Ollie, though, was not happy at all. He muttered a few curses and kicked a clod of dirt. He obviously wanted to head for the Palace, but the storage shed was holding him there like a magnet. Mr. Fairfield must have given him firm orders not to move from that spot no matter what.

But after a bit, the commotion in the main building was too much to let go. Ollie let out a throaty grumble and darted off to see what was going on.

Martin waited until he couldn't hear the footsteps, counted to five, then dashed over to Ollie's post at the rolling shed gate and pulled out a handful of keys to try in the padlock. But when he looked down at the lock, his heart skipped a beat. No keyhole—it was a combination lock!

Exhaling heavily, he started pacing around like an ornery lion in a cage. Now what? If he couldn't think of a quick way into that shed . . .

All of a sudden, it dawned on him: there was a back door! He'd seen his dad go in there once but had forgotten all about it.

He raced around to the back of the building and went straight up to the narrow door in the center of the wall. It didn't surprise him to find it locked, but that didn't worry him too much, since he was the Master of the Keys.

He pulled out the keys and tried them, one by one. *Not that one . . . Nope, not this one . . . Most of these don't even go in.*

His spirits started to sink as he got down to the last key. He held it up right in front of his nose and gritted his teeth.

"Come on, come on," he whispered intensely, as though he could make it fit by sheer will. Then he pushed the key against the slot.

No go: it wouldn't even slide in.

Martin let out a groan and looked all around, scouring his brain for an idea. He spotted a pile of metal scaffolding pieces neatly stacked against the shed wall and immediately knew what he had to do. He picked up a cross brace, jammed the flat end into the doorjamb, and pried with all his might.

Being a scrawny kid had never been a picnic for Martin, but right now his gangly body and pencil arms were his worst enemy. Though he pushed and pried with everything he had, the blasted door wouldn't budge. He could feel the blood rushing to his face, and his legs started shaking from the strain. But he kept on pulling.

Suddenly, his mind flashed to that horrible sight from his dream—the bright lights, the deafening music, the teeming crowd—and poor Rufus, straining against the heavy chains as his heartless keepers shot thousands of volts through him.

As though all that energy were now surging into his own body, Martin let out a fierce growl and gave one mighty heave worthy of a linebacker. *Crack!* The jamb splintered and the door popped open.

He rushed inside the shed and flipped on the light—and what he saw in the middle of the hard cement floor made him sick to his stomach. Rufus was lying there on his side, tightly wrapped from head to toe in a heavy tarp. He couldn't see, and he couldn't move.

"Rufus!" Martin exclaimed. "Oh, *man* . . ." Hearing his friend's voice, Rufus grunted and squirmed excitedly.

"Shhhh, keep still."

Martin wasn't sure how much time he had left, but he wasted none of it in untying the sturdy cords that held the tarp snugly around Rufus. He quickly got the tarp loose enough for his big friend to wriggle out and scramble to his feet. Thrilled to be free again, he bobbed and danced like a sprightly parakeet, slowing down just long enough to slap his long, clammy tongue across Martin's neck. Martin smiled and gave him a quick hug.

"Okay, okay. C'mon, we've gotta go!"

He rushed out the back door, and Rufus followed—but stopped short of the door. The big dino swayed back and forth nervously.

"What's the matter? Come on!"

Rufus still wouldn't move forward, so Martin pretended to run off into the night without him. That did the trick: Rufus lowered his head and lunged forward through the doorway. But the reason he had hesitated instantly became clear.

It was a very narrow door, and Rufus wasn't just a puny little lizard anymore. *Whoomp!* He got himself lodged firmly in the doorjamb. He kicked and thrashed, but he was really stuck in there tight. Martin tried to pull him through, but there was no way to get a good grip. So he squirmed underneath Rufus back into the shed and started *pushing.*

Even in the best of conditions, moving a four-hundred-pound dinosaur through a two-foot-wide door is no stroll in the park. And Martin knew two things: (1) they had very little time, and (2) they were making way too much noise. But he also knew that failure was out of the question. So he pushed and pushed, his face turning purple and his eyes bugging out, as Rufus kept pedaling away against the slippery floor. But he would not budge.

Panting hard, Martin looked all around the shed. He noticed a bunch of restaurant supplies in a corner and raced over to have a closer look. Right there on a shelf, glowing like gold, were several big plastic jugs of cooking oil.

He grabbed a jug, hauled it over to Rufus, and got right to work. On most days he would have had a very tough time lifting a heavy thing like that, but right now he was running on high adrenaline; he skillfully hoisted it up onto his shoulder and poured the oil right over the stubborn spot where wood met dino skin.

He ran around and did the same on the other side,

then skittered back behind Rufus for another push. Again Rufus pedaled his feet, and again Martin shoved with everything he had.

"Come on, *come on* . . . "

Still, no forward motion was happening.

Martin jumped up on Rufus's back and whispered intensely in his ear cavity.

"You *have to do this,* Rufus. It's your only chance. They're gonna chain you up and zap you and make you dance in front of a whole bunch of grubby tourists. I know you can do it, boy. *Please,* just do it. Push. *Push!*"

All of a sudden Rufus let out a loud bark and gave a mighty lurch forward—and *squotch!* He squirted free, stumbling out into the great outdoors. Martin fell off him onto the grass and rolled over onto his knees.

"Yeah! You did it, buddy! Woo-hoo!"

When he heard his voice echo back to him from the woods, he winced. Too loud!

"Let's go!" he half whispered.

Rufus followed Martin along the fence toward the back of the main building, letting out a braying noise as they ran.

"Shhhhhh!" Martin cautioned.

They quickly made it to the service gate—but there was no sign of Audrey.

Now his worst fears started rearing up again. Maybe she had gotten lost in there and couldn't find her way back. Or maybe—he tried not to entertain the thought, but it kept butting in—maybe she got caught. *Aaacch!* Martin knew he would have to go in and find out.

He went over to the restaurant kitchen window, took a deep breath, and started to climb in—when Audrey suddenly appeared on the other side, startling him.

"Hoh!"

"Sorry. All *right*! You got him!" she said brightly as she climbed out. "Hiya, Rufus!"

"Did they see you?"

"I don't think so."

"Great job. How did you . . ." He peered through the window and could see, through a narrow opening leading from the restaurant into the midway, two men scrambling around in confusion—Ollie and Jasper. It looked like they were trying to grab something small, prickly, and really fast.

"I let the muskrats out."

Martin looked at her and couldn't help smiling. They started to laugh, but it ended quickly when Rufus let out a high-pitched squeal.

"Come on," Martin said as he dug the keys out of his pockets and started trying them in the gate padlock.

This time, luck was on his side: it took only three keys to find the one that opened the lock. He pulled off the chain, and he and Audrey rolled the gate open. He dumped the rest of the keys on the ground, and the three of them clambered up the ridge and into the woods.

Martin felt a huge wave of relief—and maybe just a bit of pride—rushing through him as they pushed ahead into the predawn darkness of the forest. Mr. Eckhart lived way on the other side of town, but getting to his house should be a piece of cake compared to what they'd just pulled off. Yep, the hardest part was definitely over.

Right?

# SIXTEEN

It was quite a sight: two nervous eleven-year-olds and a tall T. rex thrashing their way through the woods. Or it would have been a sight, if it had been light enough for anybody to see them. That possibility was growing by the minute, as they could tell from the hints of dawn peeking up over the eastern horizon.

"Are you sure this is the way?" Audrey asked more than once. She'd never been in this part of the woods before.

"I said I'm sure," Martin said, although he could tell his *un*sure tone wasn't giving her much comfort.

After a good mile and a half of stumbling and groping their way along, they finally came out of the woods near the edge of town. It was a quiet neighborhood with small, ordinary-looking homes, not yet stirring with signs of daily life.

Martin led the way up the embankment to a road, and they made their way along the grassy shoulder for about three blocks. Arriving at an intersection, they stopped and Martin took a moment to think. He tried hard to look like he knew what to do next.

"Which way?" Audrey said.

Martin looked all around. "Over there."

They started across the street, but when they got halfway across there was a flash of light that stopped them in their tracks. They looked down the road and saw a pair of headlights, closing in fast. Without a moment's thought, Martin and Audrey doubled back to the side of the road and ducked behind a big juniper bush.

But not Rufus. He stood there in the middle of the street, transfixed by the sight of those two fiery balls of light coming around the curve, getting closer and closer.

"Rufus!" Martin called. "Rufus! Come here!"

But the big dino didn't move. He was frozen there like . . . well, like an animal caught in headlights.

Martin and Audrey sprinted out from behind the bush and into the road to grab Rufus. They pulled hard, and Rufus somehow got the message that he needed to move. He went along with them back to their roadside hiding place—just an instant before a big panel truck finished rounding the curve and shot right past.

Rufus had never seen anything quite like that before—and it got him good and spooked. He hissed and twitched, ready to bolt.

"Shhhhh," said Martin, stroking his back gently. "Easy, boy."

"Ai-yai-yai," Audrey rasped. "Do you think they saw?"

Martin watched the truck disappear down the street. "Nah. They probably would have crashed or something." He took a breath, then looked over at the reddening eastern horizon. "Let's go."

Again they headed out into the road, this time making it across without any unwanted adventures. They moved silently into the neighborhood and after about two blocks stopped in front of a small house. Martin scanned it, a blank look on his face.

"This one?" Audrey asked.

Martin nodded.

"Are you sure?"

"Yeah."

"You don't look sure."

"I rode right by here last week, and he was mowing his lawn. It's this one."

Audrey scratched her neck and fidgeted. "Okay. Let's go, then."

"Wait. It might be that one."

"Martin!"

"No! This one. I'm positive."

"No you're not."

"What do you mean?"

"You just said it might be that one."

"It's not. It's this one."

"How do you know?"

"Because I'm positive."

"If you were positive, you wouldn't have said it might be that one."

"I didn't make that as a positive statement."

"Which statement?"

"The other one."

*"What?"*

Rufus let out a throaty bark. "Shhhhh!" they both hissed at him—even though their own bickering was probably noisier.

A few house lights were on in the neighborhood, and Martin knew that if anybody was looking out their window right now, the sight of two kids with a nervous tyrannosaur was sure to set off a few alarm bells.

Across the street, somebody's garage door started opening.

"In the back," said Martin. "Hurry up." He trotted up the driveway of the house they'd been staring at, and Audrey and Rufus fell in behind him. They circled around to the backyard, where, Martin assumed, they'd be less likely to be seen.

When they got there, Martin stopped again to think. He felt nervous being in somebody's backyard uninvited (especially if it was the wrong one!), and

Audrey's staring at him just made it worse. Rufus seemed nervous too—he swayed back and forth and gave a restless snort.

Deciding he'd have to go for it, Martin stepped up to the back door of the house and knocked. No sign of life inside. He peeked through the window into the darkness inside, then knocked louder. Either nobody was home, or somebody was fast asleep.

He took hold of the knob and gave it a turn—and was a bit surprised when the door opened. Audrey held her breath as he took a step inside.

"Hello?" he called. "Mr. Eckhart?"

Still no answer. "Ohhhh, wow," Audrey mumbled. "Oh, wow. I knew this was the wrong one. I knew it. I had this feeling about it, and—"

Seeing something, she froze.

"What." Martin came back out and looked at what she was staring at: on the other side of the patio, behind a rusty old deck chair, was that odd-looking Van de Graaff generator Mr. Eckhart had brought to school last spring.

Martin gave her a self-satisfied little grin; of *course* it was the right house. She almost rolled her eyes, but he could tell she was more relieved than peeved.

There was a small garage at the back end of the driveway, and Audrey went over to check it out. She pulled on the handle at the bottom of the door, and it swung open. "His car is gone."

Martin took a second to process this. "He must have stayed at the U overnight."

"Why is it taking him so *long*?"

They both jumped as Rufus let out a growl and leaped halfway across the yard.

"Rufus!" Audrey scolded. "Be quiet! Come back here."

When Rufus turned back toward them, they could see right away what had set him off: he threw his head back, snapped his jaws a few times like an alligator— and swallowed the last bit of a furry gray tail.

"Ai-yai-yai," Audrey droned. "Poor squirrel . . ."

"He's really hungry."

Audrey scratched her elbow and let out a nervous sigh. "We can't stay here, Martin. Somebody's gonna see."

Martin looked up one more time at the brightening sky, and tried to put it all together. "We'll have to stay in there till he gets back." He nodded toward the garage.

"In *there*? Really?"

"Unless you have a better idea."

She looked at him blankly. "Okay. Let's go."

"Rufus!" Martin gave a half whistle and headed for the garage; Rufus followed without complaining. They all went inside, and Martin turned on the light as Audrey pulled the door down behind them.

Now all they could do was wait. But the dead quiet that engulfed them allowed all kinds of worrisome thoughts to intrude into Martin's head as he paced slowly around the room.

He looked at his watch: almost seven o'clock. By

now his parents were certainly up and had discovered his empty bed. They'd scrambled all over the place looking for him, then probably called the police.

Ollie, or maybe somebody else, had surely noticed the broken back door on the maintenance shed. No doubt they'd called Ben Fairfield, and he'd probably yelled at a bunch of people and then sent out a search party of his own.

The school day would be starting soon, and two seventh-grade desks would be unoccupied.

Martin sank down onto the cold cement floor. He rubbed his eyes, then watched absently as Audrey gently stroked Rufus's belly, trying to keep him calm. But she didn't look very calm herself.

"Are you okay?" he asked.

"Do you have your phone?"

He felt in his pocket. Nope: forgotten again. He looked at her and shook his head.

Her eyebrows knotted up, and she looked down at the floor. "Jade and my dad'll be going crazy. I should've left a note or something."

"Yeah . . . me too," he offered, barely above a whisper.

Maybe the hard part really was still to come.

# SEVENTEEN

Martin had been pacing back and forth in that tiny garage for what seemed like forever. Audrey stood leaning against a wall, bouncing an old rubber ball she had found on the floor. Rufus twitched and fidgeted, giving an occasional squeal or low gurgle, or sometimes scratching the side of his head against the wall.

The *plop, plop, plop* of the ball on the floor was really starting to get on Martin's already-frazzled nerves.

"Do you think you could, sort of like, not do that?"

"Do what?"

He let out a sigh and stepped over to the small window in the side wall for about the forty-sixth time. It was hard to see much from that angle, but there was a sliver of a view of the street out front. A car went by, and though he couldn't be completely sure, to Martin it looked a lot like a police cruiser.

"There goes another one."

"They must be looking all over the place," Audrey observed.

Martin scratched his knee. "What time is it now?"

She checked her watch. "Ten-thirty."

"What's taking him so *long*?" he grumbled, resuming his pacing. For Mr. Eckhart to be gone that long—*overnight,* even—was not a good sign, not good at all.

Martin was regretting having skipped dinner the night before; now he was feeling plenty hungry. And he knew they'd both have to hit the bathroom pretty soon. And if that wasn't enough, Rufus was getting more restless by the minute.

Some unsettling thoughts crept into Martin's head. *Is this really the best plan? What if Mr. Eckhart doesn't come back at all? Or if he does, how do we know he won't be just like all the others and sell Rufus up the river?* Stop! You can't think like that! . . . *Or is it possible they're right, and Rufus will soon be too big and too mean to handle, even for me, and he'll have to be in a cage?*

"No! That's not it!"

Martin had blurted it out before he realized it.

Audrey looked at him like he was some lunatic from Pluto.

"Sorry," he mumbled. "I was just . . ."

"Are you okay?"

"Yeah. Sorry." He cleared his throat and took a deep breath. *No, this is the plan, and it's definitely the right one. And it's too late to turn back anyway.*

Suddenly, Rufus lunged at an old tire in the corner and chomped down on it like it was a giant ham sandwich.

"Rufus, no!" Martin scolded. "That's *yecch*."

"He's really, really hungry," Audrey added, in case Martin hadn't noticed.

Martin thought hard. "Maybe there's some meat in the house."

"Okay."

They went over to the small door in the back, but it was locked tight. So they went to the big car-entry door and Martin tilted it up just an inch or two while Audrey put her cheek to the ground and peeked out.

"Looks clear."

Martin lifted the door a bit higher, and Rufus sprang over to be the first one out.

"Rufus, *no*," Audrey chided. "Just us. You wait here."

He stared at them with a menacing leer as Martin held the door just a foot or so off the ground, and he and Audrey slipped underneath it. Rufus ducked down and tried to follow them, pushing his head against the door. But they both pushed back from outside.

"Rufus, *wait*," Martin said firmly. "We'll be right back."

The door was heavy enough that they could get it closed before Rufus could squirt through. Then they trotted across the patio and went in the back door of the house, into the kitchen.

When they opened the fridge, some of the sights and smells that came out almost made them gag.

"Ewww, look at *that* one," said Audrey, pointing to a purplish lump in a back corner. "He must be doing some of his science experiments in here."

"I don't see any meat," said Martin.

"Maybe there was some, but it mutated into something else."

"Wait . . . what about this?" He unwrapped the aluminum foil from a brownish chunk of something and took a sniff. They both studied it closely.

"Meat loaf?"

"I'm thinking yeah. Let's go."

They made a beeline for the door, but Audrey stopped short.

"Oh!" She pointed to a phone sitting on the counter. "I'm gonna call Daddy and tell him we're okay."

She reached for the phone, but Martin had a thought. "Wait. He'll see the number, and they'll figure out where we are."

Grimly, she took her hand off the phone.

They both stiffened as there was a *thunk* outside. At first Martin thought maybe Rufus was up to some kind of mischief, but then he realized the sound was a car door shutting, and it came from the front of the house, not the back.

"Mr. Eckhart! He's back!" Audrey exclaimed.

Now smiling, they ran for the door again, but Martin grabbed her arm and they froze once more as there was a second *thunk* . . . then a third . . . then a fourth. Something was not right.

There were voices outside. Adult voices. And they seemed pretty worked up.

Wriggling his fingers nervously, Martin tiptoed across the room and slowly peeked around into the living room. He flinched and pulled back as there was a loud banging on the front door.

"Hello!" came a familiar voice. "Sheriff's department. Anyone home?" *Bang bang bang bang!*

"How did they know?" Audrey whispered intensely.

"I might have mentioned Mr. Eckhart . . ."

She winced as Sheriff Grimes banged on the door one more time; then the voices started up again. There must have been seven or eight of them out there. One of the voices—the one that seemed most agitated of all—belonged to Ben Fairfield.

Some of the people outside started walking up the driveway. Martin and Audrey ducked down low, making sure they'd be out of sight in case anybody got the idea to peek in any windows. But now Martin recognized two more voices—his own parents!

He and Audrey scurried over to the back door, stooped low, and pushed the curtain aside just enough to see Martin's mom and dad arriving in the back-yard with a pair of deputies. They explored the yard and patio, as though they were somehow expecting

Martin, Audrey, and Rufus to just drop out of the big oak tree in the middle of the yard.

Then they gathered right next to the garage and started talking. His dad was only three feet away from the small window on the side of the garage.

Martin squeezed his eyes shut and put his hands over his ears, as though that would somehow make him and Audrey—and Rufus—invisible. "Please be quiet, Rufus," he whispered. "Please be quiet, please be quiet . . ."

When he opened his eyes again, he saw the others still standing there—nobody had thought to look through that garage window.

But now there were some loud footsteps headed straight for the kitchen door. Martin and Audrey plastered themselves low against the wall, holding their breath.

*Bang bang bang bang!* "Peter Eckhart, please come to the door." It was Ben Fairfield, and he was right above them, just outside. *Bang bang bang!*

Martin and Audrey looked up and saw the door-knob start to turn.

"We can't just walk in there, Ben." Sheriff Grimes's voice seemed to come from nowhere.

"Who says so?"

"We've gotta have a warrant. It's the law, buddy."

"Here's my warrant."

With impossibly quick reflexes, Audrey snapped her hand up and gave the locking switch in the door-knob a little twist. The knob rattled back and forth, and then the whole door shook loudly. It seemed like it might come loose from its hinges.

"I'm telling you, Ben. Can't do it," Sheriff Grimes insisted.

"There's nobody here, Ben," Mr. Tinker called from across the patio. "Let's go, they can't have gotten far."

Martin and Audrey sat there, stone still, as the footsteps headed back down the driveway, the grumbling voices faded, car doors slammed, and at least three vehicles drove off.

By some miracle, Rufus never made a peep.

The two of them sat there for a good five minutes, not daring to move, or even speak. Finally, Martin got up and slipped quietly into the living room. He made his way across the room and carefully peeked out a small window next to the front door, scanning as much of the yard as he could see, then jogged back into the kitchen.

"They're gone. Let's go."

He picked up the foil-wrapped chunk and they headed out the back door.

"How do we know they won't come back?" Audrey said as they crossed the patio toward the garage.

"We just have to hope Mr. Eckhart gets here first."

"That could take hours. Days, even."

"It's not that far. Anyway, he's supposed to be at class today."

"I don't know, Martin. Maybe we should . . . think of something else or something."

"What else can we do, Audrey? The whole town is

probably looking for us," Martin said, pulling up on the garage door handle.

"I'm just trying to help. You don't have to get all snippy."

"I'm not being snippy."

"Yes you are. Snippy, snippy."

"I'm not snippy, all I'm saying—"

*Bang!* The door suddenly flew all the way open, nearly lifting Martin off the ground with it. They both watched, dumbfounded, as Rufus—having rammed into the door in just the right spot and at just the right moment—shot out of the garage and took off down the driveway.

Aghast, Audrey and Martin stood there rigidly, watching their big dinosaur scamper off like a school kid on recess. For a good five seconds they just stood with their mouths hanging open.

*"Noooooooooo!"* they bellowed in unison, then sprinted after him. But by the time they got to the end of the driveway, Rufus was already halfway down the block.

*"Rufus, stop!"* Martin hollered.

*"Rufuuus!"* Audrey cried. But their desperate calls seemed to evaporate in the cool morning air.

They kept after him as best they could, but Rufus was a faster runner than they were, and soon he was a good two blocks ahead of them. He turned a corner onto another street, and now Martin was starting to worry that they might actually lose sight of him. And even worse, somebody was going to see him now for sure.

Martin felt about a dozen knots forming just below his diaphragm. "Oh, man . . . oh, man . . . oh, man . . ."

When they got to the corner, they stopped and looked down the street where Rufus had gone. No sign of him.

"Ai-yai-yai-yai-*yai*," Audrey moaned.

They charged ahead, desperately looking in all directions. Then Martin stopped in his tracks.

"There!"

Just a few houses up the street, there was Rufus, intently sniffing at a plastic flamingo in somebody's front yard. He seemed not to know whether to eat it, make friends with it, or run the other way.

"Rufus, come here!" Martin shouted, and he and Audrey ran straight toward him. But he didn't seem to hear them at all; deciding the big pink bird must be breakfast, he clamped his teeth down on it, jerked it out of the ground, and started chewing.

Then he was startled by a sharp *yapping* sound. He spat out the flamingo and spun around to see a little gray Scottish terrier, barking furiously at this alien beast in his yard. The dog danced and darted around, seeming to want to charge Rufus—but making it a point not to get *too* close.

"Rufus, come! Now!" Audrey called as she and Martin finally made it to the yard. But Rufus's eyes were fixed on the annoying little creature at his feet—and his predatory instincts kicked right in. Spreading his jaws wide, he let out a giant *hiss* and lunged at the dog, who promptly took off in the other direction.

*"No!"* Martin and Audrey both shouted as the Scottie flew up onto the porch and—just as Rufus snapped his jaws shut with a loud *thwock!*—barely escaped into the house through a doggie door.

"Holy mama," Martin rasped.

Now the front door of the house opened and a lady in giant hair curlers and an avocado face mask stepped out. "Fritzie, what on earth is going on out—" Seeing the tall beast standing only three feet away, staring coldly at her, she froze.

Everybody—including Rufus—stood there, rock-still. Martin dreaded the thought of what would come next. And after three seconds, he found out: the lady let out an eardrum-shattering SCREAM that they could probably hear all the way in Milwaukee.

The sound so alarmed Rufus that he hopped back, slipped on the porch step, and lurched face-first into a big American flag hanging on the post.

"No, Rufus, no!" Martin cried out, but he and Audrey could only stand there like rusted robots as Rufus stumbled back out into the yard, blinded by the flag that had come loose and was now draped over his head. The lady kept screaming as she retreated back inside and slammed the door—though it was still loud and clear as she kept carrying on in there.

Martin and Audrey tried to grab at the flag, but now Rufus was in an all-out panic, jerking around every which way. His foot landed on a tricycle, which shot out from under him—and he went airborne like an Olympic diver, hitting the ground flat on his side with a resounding *thud.*

Audrey grimaced. "Oooooooh, *ow!*"

"*Please,* Rufus," Martin cried hoarsely, trying vainly to get his arms around him. "You're only making it worse!"

Luckily, the flag came off as Rufus struggled to his feet. But now he was even more shaken up than before.

He darted out of the yard and straight into the street—just as a big green Land Rover zoomed up. The car came to a screeching, swerving stop, barely missing him. Rufus jumped up in the air, gave a husky bark, and took off down the street as fast as his beefy legs would carry him.

"No!" Martin yelled one more time. He could feel his thigh muscles burning as he desperately tried to keep up. "Come back!"

The man driving the car jumped out and stared, slack-jawed, as Rufus charged down the road. The lady in the house was now leaning out an upstairs window, hollering "Call the police! Somebody call the police!"

None of which was doing a darn thing to slow down Rufus—who was now charging straight toward the center of town.

## EIGHTEEN

Gage Park was a pleasant little patch of grass and trees where, on a normal day, you might see kids playing tag, couples holding hands, or older folks standing in the middle of the park admiring the statue of Philippe Dumont, an old-time explorer looking gallant on his high-stepping horse.

There were no people in the park this morning, but a few dozen pigeons were making themselves right at home on the statue when a very large, very agitated creature came bounding on the scene, with two equally unnerved young humans following not too far behind.

"Rufus, you have to *stop*!" Martin called.

Rufus lunged at the pigeons, and Martin and Audrey had to duck as they were suddenly surrounded by a cloud of flapping, fluttering birds. Rufus slashed and snapped at them, but somehow they all managed to escape.

Flustered, Rufus jumped at the statue, chomping right down on the leg of Monsieur Dumont's horse.

"Get away from there, you big bonehead!" Audrey hollered.

"Shhhh! You're making it worse," said Martin.

He tentatively reached toward the twitchy dino. "Rufus, calm *down,*" he said, stroking Rufus's left thigh as though he were a skittish stallion. Rufus let go of the statue—though his eyes were still blazing. For just a fleeting moment, Martin was afraid maybe those teeth were about to be turned on him and Audrey. But Rufus actually did start to calm down a bit, or at least, he didn't seem like he was ready to bolt again.

"That's it, good boy."

"Now what?" Audrey said.

Martin looked all around. "If we can . . . there's a shortcut. We can get back to the garage."

"Okay," Audrey said, though she sounded pretty unsure.

"Come on," Martin said, trying to act like it was all under control.

They had barely gotten to the edge of the park when they spotted something and stopped cold. Just a half block ahead, a dark Lincoln crawled along like a prowling panther, then came to a stop. Martin stood there, paralyzed. He knew whose car it was.

The passenger door opened, and out stepped a familiar but unwelcome face: Ollie Thwait, the Trout

Palace guard. He scowled at them as the driver's-side door opened and a man with a gleaming bald pate got out, throwing them a menacing glare of his own. In one hand, Ben Fairfield had a walkie-talkie. He reached back into the car with the other and pulled out a long, dark object that Martin recognized instantly: another tranquilizing rifle.

Rufus must have recognized it too, because he jerked and grunted testily. Martin's heart rose directly into his throat.

"Ai-yai-yai," Audrey squeaked as Mr. Fairfield raised the walkie-talkie and growled into the mouthpiece, loud and clear.

"Frank."

"Yeah, Ben," said the sheriff's crackly voice at the other end.

"Found 'em. Gage Park, on Chestnut."

"Roger that."

Almost instantly, a siren started wailing in the distance.

Something about the sound set off a voice in Martin's head, telling him they were done and it was time to give up. But as Ben Fairfield slowly lifted the rifle to his shoulder and took aim at Rufus, an even louder voice inside yelled, *Stop standing there, you idiot! Get moving!*

"This way!" Martin exclaimed, taking off across the street at full tilt. Catching his energy, Audrey and Rufus followed.

Mr. Fairfield and Ollie tore after them, leaving the

car sitting in the middle of the street, as Martin led Rufus and Audrey into an alley between two small buildings. They could hear Fairfield barking into the walkie-talkie behind them.

"Cutting across to Green Bay, heading east now. Got it, Frank? Cut 'em off!"

Any thought Martin had of making it back to Mr. Eckhart's garage was now a distant memory. Their only remaining hope was to somehow get out of there without getting caught. Maybe they could make it back to the woods and be safe there.

They came out the other end of the alley and found themselves right where they didn't want to be: on Green Bay Avenue, the busiest street in town.

Leading the way, Martin made a mad dash down the street, and people turned to look. At first they stayed strangely calm, as though what they were watching was some kind of bizarre street theater. When Fairfield and Ollie came barreling out of the alley, even that didn't cause any particular alarm. But when Rufus ran by an orange-haired lady and chomped the leather purse right out of her hand, she let out a hellacious *shriek!*

That was everybody's cue to push the panic button.

Murmurs turned to screams. Drivers slammed on their brakes, causing three fender benders within seconds. Horns honked chaotically. Little kids screamed and cried as their parents tried to sweep them as far away as possible from this ferocious-looking creature on the loose.

Some people craned their necks to get a better look; others just sprinted right out of there.

Dogs barked up a storm. A guy on a motorcycle twisted his head around to check out Rufus—and took a fast header right into Tom Reavis Memorial Fountain.

Now, on top of everything else, Martin was afraid somebody might really get hurt. He felt like they had all been transported into one of those scary monster-on-the-loose movies, and Rufus was the monster. But Rufus wasn't attacking anyone—all he was doing was *running*. Martin just wanted to shout, *Everybody calm down! Everything's okay!*

But for him and Audrey and Rufus, everything was definitely *not* okay. They felt themselves slowing down, and Ben Fairfield and Ollie, showing remarkable stamina for guys their age, were gaining on them.

A police cruiser, seeming to come out of nowhere, skidded to a halt just ahead of them. Now they were completely cut off. Martin looked all around, desperate for an escape route.

"Through there!" he shouted, pointing to a storefront across the street. He darted between two parked cars and raced across. Audrey and Rufus fell in right behind.

Mr. Fairfield took off after them, followed by Ollie and the officer from the squad car.

"What, through *there*?" Audrey rasped as they raced toward a row of shops.

"I've been in there. There's a service door in back," Martin said. "We can make it to the woods." He ran right up to the front entrance of the Spotted Otter, a big gift shop that was popular with tourists, and the automated front doors slid open. "Duck, Rufus!"

Rufus lowered his head, and the three of them rushed inside.

The place was packed from wall to wall with mugs, glass figurines, painted plates, cuckoo clocks, porcelain dolls, and thousands of other delicate knickknacks. So Martin and Audrey had to slow down and be extra careful as they led Rufus through the narrow center aisle, skillfully guiding him between the high shelves of pretty breakables.

"Sorry . . . sorry," Audrey and Martin muttered as they made their way past the customers, who stood there, rigid and bug-eyed.

Somehow, the three of them made it to the far end of the store without bumping a single item out of place—until, at the very end, the tiniest tip of Rufus's tail caught a little glass globe, knocking it off a shelf. But as before, Audrey's reflexes were lightning-quick—she stretched out and caught it just before it took a shattering nosedive.

They raced straight past a petrified lady at a rear checkout counter ("Sorry," Martin said sheepishly), barreled into the storage room, and immediately spotted the service door in the back wall. Only one thought ran through Martin's head: *Please, please don't be locked!*

As he reached for the bar handle, a loud CRASH made them all jump. They looked back through the opening into the main store to see Ben Fairfield, Ollie, and the deputy in a tangled mess in the center aisle. The tranquilizing gun had caught on a post and all three of them had slammed into each other, tumbling against a shelf and sending glass souvenirs cascading down on them from all sides. The shelf tipped over and started a chain reaction of collapsing shelves and flying glassware, leaving the hapless customers scrambling to get out of the way.

When the poor lady behind the counter saw what was happening to her store, her jaw sagged, her eyes rolled up—and she dropped straight to the floor.

"Holy mama," Martin muttered.

"She's okay," said Audrey as the lady made it back to her knees. "Keep going, Martin. *Go!*"

Martin grabbed the bar and pushed—and was hugely relieved when the big door swung open. Maybe, he dared to think as they ran outside, with their pursuers hung up now, they might actually have a chance . . . ?

They ran down a short stretch of alley and came out on Elm Street, which wasn't quite as crowded as Green Bay, but the furor that erupted there was exactly the same.

They hadn't gotten far when the sound of screeching tires startled them. Down toward the end of the block, a pickup truck skidded to a halt, narrowly missing a panicky tourist. The driver and passenger jumped out, and Martin knew exactly who it was before their feet even hit the ground.

"Martin! Hold up!" Mr. Tinker shouted. He and Mrs. Tinker charged toward them, struggling against the flow of fleeing people.

But Martin did not want to give up, not to his parents, not to anybody. He and his loyal companions turned and ran one more time, heading down still another street as Ben Fairfield and his crew, having extracted themselves from the Spotted Otter, appeared again.

The three fugitives kept on running straight through the heart of Menominee Springs, causing a sensation everywhere they went, and somehow staying ahead of the posse chasing after them. They ran past St. Jude's Church, kept on going past the fancy houses on Chelten Lane, and cut diagonally across Pfister Park.

By the time they were running past Menominee Springs Middle School—where they were *supposed* to be this morning—their tanks were just about empty.

"Martin," Audrey wheezed, "I can't run anymore. We can't make it. Maybe we better—"

"No!" Martin snapped, although he was every bit as spent as she was. "We have to keep going!" By now any actual plan or expectation of a real escape no longer existed in Martin's brain. They had to keep going because . . . well, because they just *had* to.

Sheriff Grimes's squad car came to a stop just a half block ahead, cutting them off yet again. They looked back the way they had come: Mr. Fairfield's gang was bearing down on them. *Fast.*

There was only one way out, and Martin didn't hesitate. "Through here," he panted, and they scurried through the gate onto the school's athletic field.

As they chugged across the field, lungs aflame, feet heavy as anvils, Martin's mind started to drift. Time seemed to wind down to a crawl, and he felt like he was running in slow motion through empty space. The only sounds he could hear were his own labored breathing and throbbing heartbeat. *How did it come to this? I'm just a regular kid, trying to help a defenseless animal. Why is everybody treating us like criminals?*

He thought of the seventh-grade classroom across the way, where right now Mrs. Sanders was probably quizzing the class on math or geography or grammar, with empty chairs where he and Audrey would normally be. Did anybody realize they weren't there? Did they even care? Didn't they know how important it was to save Rufus from a terrible life under the thumb of Ben Fairfield?

Martin's eyes drifted over to the school building and fixed on the row of open classroom windows. Was that Donald Grimes pointing at them through the window, jumping up and down and shouting something to the rest of the class?

"Get away from us! We're just trying to help him! Go away!"

*Wait a minute.* It was Donald, all right, but it wasn't his voice.

Snapping out of his dreamy state, Martin realized the voice was Audrey's, and she was shouting at Ben Fairfield's gang and the police officers who were now right on top of them.

The three of them had made it to the far end of the field, but they came to a skidding stop in a corner of a high, unforgiving chain-link fence. The gate Martin had been hoping to fly through was locked tight. They were trapped. No place left to run.

Fairfield and his men quickly surrounded them, and Ben raised his dart rifle. Sheriff Grimes had one too, and he struggled to load in a cartridge.

Rufus seemed to know what was coming, and he danced and growled menacingly.

"All right, you kids," Mr. Fairfield wheezed, "you had your fun. Now get away from the animal."

"You can't have him!" Martin yelled as he and Audrey shuffled back and forth to keep themselves between Rufus and the gun.

"He's my property. Legally bought and paid for. Now step out of there."

"We're not moving!" Audrey snapped.

Mr. Fairfield tried to follow Rufus's movements with the rifle, but he couldn't get off a shot without risking hitting one of his human protectors.

Now Martin's mom and dad caught up with the group and rushed straight at the cornered trio.

"Martin, what in the bloody blazes are you doing?" Mr. Tinker hollered.

Rufus let out a growl and went into a menacing crouch, causing them to quickly back away and take a safer spot behind Mr. Fairfield.

"Martin, you come away from there," Mrs. Tinker commanded. "Right now, I mean it!"

Martin felt a burning sensation in his throat that spread all the way up to his forehead. "I can't, Mom. I *can't!*"

His dad looked like he might explode at any second. "What do you mean you *can't?* You heard your mother. Get over here!"

"Look," Sheriff Grimes interjected, "just come out of there like your folks are saying, and this'll be over in a flash."

"You're not shooting him," Martin fired back, his jaw firmly set. "You'll have to shoot us first!"

"Yeah!" Audrey shouted.

"Take it down a notch, will you?" Mr. Fairfield scolded. "It's just a tranquilizing dart."

"Ben!" Mrs. Tinker snapped. "Don't you dare shoot with them there!"

"I've got this, Ann," Fairfield said, still trying to get a good aim. "You need to stay out of it."

"Really, Ben? I'm thinking *you* need to stay out of it."

There was a commotion across the field, and everybody looked over to see a mob of middle-schoolers running toward them. Martin and Audrey recognized them immediately: their seventh-grade classmates. They were completely ignoring Mrs. Sanders, who was chasing after them with a look of utter horror on her face.

"No, no, no! We cannot come out here! Everybody back inside, *now*! Michael! Hannah, no! Oh, dear lord . . ."

"Whoa, hold on there!" the sheriff shouted, suddenly awakened to the situation. "You kids stay back. *Back!*" He and his men did their best to herd the group away from Rufus, and it turned out he didn't need much help: Rufus suddenly hissed and snapped at the approaching mob, sending everybody into a quick about-face. Some screams and yips flew out of the crowd, and Martin threw his arm in front of Rufus. "Shhh, shhh, shhh, steady . . ."

The kids didn't retreat far; they turned right back around again, pressing against the thin line of policemen's arms holding them back.

In the middle of the pack, Donald Grimes jumped up and down, pointing furiously at Rufus. "There, see what I mean? I'm not crazy! I told you! I *told* you!"

Mrs. Sanders turned around and raced back toward the building, struggling to make headway in her high heels. "Mr. Clayborne! Mr. Clayborne!"

"Hey, Martin," Max Mitchell called out. "Is that really a *dinosaur*?"

"Where'd you guys get that?" said Alyssa Belden.

"Does he bite?" said Michael Tripp.

"No. Well . . ." Martin felt a bit thrown by the

sudden burst of attention from his classmates. It felt really odd having all those eyes zeroed in on him, and it was distracting him from protecting Rufus. Trying to focus, he kept shuffling back and forth with Audrey to block Ben Fairfield's aim. They jumped up and down too, waving their arms.

"Frank," Ben said impatiently to Sheriff Grimes, "are you gonna get those two out of there, or what?"

The sheriff looked lost, and so did his deputies. He didn't have a good angle to shoot from either, and obviously had no desire to get any closer to Rufus. Finally, he took a halfhearted step forward.

"He's in a really bad mood," Martin warned.

"Yeah. And hungry," Audrey said.

That stopped the sheriff cold. The seventh graders chuckled edgily, but it turned to worried murmurs as he put down his tranquilizing gun and reached for his revolver.

"No, you're not doing that!" Mr. Fairfield snapped.

"Whoa, whoa, whoa!" Mr. Tinker shouted at the same time.

"Frank, no!" Mrs. Tinker yelled.

"Well, what the heck do you expect me—"

"Ah, for crying out loud!" Ben barked. "You guys do it."

He was talking to Ollie and his other henchman, Jasper. Caught off guard, they stood there, and the color drained from their faces.

"What are you waiting for?" Fairfield growled. "Go!"

Ollie and Jasper must have found Mr. Fairfield

even scarier than Rufus, because now they started edging toward Martin and Audrey—who took a step back, even closer to their restive companion. Rufus leered at the slowly approaching men.

Mr. Tinker was looking angry, worried, and strangely torn, all at once. "Ben, this is nuts."

"When I want your opinion, Gordon, I'll ask for it," said Mr. Fairfield, still swinging the gun back and forth, looking for an opening.

Mrs. Tinker was scowling. "Ben Fairfield, who do you think—" She cut off and let out a gasp as Rufus made a lunge at Ollie, almost taking off his hand. Amid a swell of screams and alarmed whoops from the crowd, Ollie stepped back and looked over at Ben Fairfield imploringly.

Ben let out an exasperated breath and just kept holding the gun barrel straight out in front of him. "Martin," he growled, "I'm not going to ask you again. You and your friend need to move your butts away from there *now*."

That was the first time Martin could remember Mr. Fairfield calling him by his real name—almost as though he was an actual, thinking person, not just Gordon Tinker's little kid. This caught him off guard. The rational part of his brain was telling him he should do what Mr. Fairfield said—act like a reasonable person. But another part of his brain—the angry, defiant part—was calling out pretty loudly too, and he wasn't so sure he could ignore those calls. He exchanged a glance with Audrey, and, energized by their unspoken bond of solidarity, they turned their flinty gazes back to Mr. Fairfield, standing firm.

"Gordon," said Ben Fairfield without batting an eye, "tell your kid to step away from there, and we can put an end to this."

Martin's dad stood there without saying anything. He shifted his feet and cleared his throat.

*"Gordon?"* said Ben Fairfield in a menacing drone.

Mr. Tinker pursed his lips and looked at the ground. The anger was gone from his eyes now, and he appeared more troubled and distant than anything else.

Martin wasn't sure if he was purposely ignoring Ben or what. For the first time ever, he got the sense that his dad might actually tell Ben Fairfield to take a hike.

Finally, Mr. Tinker looked back up and spoke in a quiet, almost resigned tone of voice. "Come on, Marty. Let's go."

Martin's heart sank. He felt angry, disappointed, and resentful all at once. "Why should I listen to you?"

"Look, the deed is done. It's time for you to accept it. Come away from there, before somebody really gets hurt."

All Martin's emotions were welling up to the surface. He looked at his father, jaw muscles tight, holding back the tears that were desperately trying to break through. "You never take my side, not ever! You think I don't measure up because I'm not like you. Well, maybe I don't *want* to be like you. And if you don't like that . . . well, tough cookies!"

He felt like he was standing outside himself, watching as some alien being took over his body and started saying things the real Martin never would. He braced for what he knew would come next—his dad blowing a gasket, and turning a very unpleasant scene into maybe a very scary one.

But it didn't happen. Mr. Tinker just stood there, gaping at Martin as though he were some mysterious stranger instead of his own son.

Mr. Fairfield's expression didn't change one bit. "All right, Martin, you made your point. Now step . . . away . . . from the beast."

Martin turned his angry gaze to Mr. Fairfield and spoke with the authority of an army general. "He's not a beast. His name is Rufus. I found his egg, and I raised him, and he's my friend. And the only way you're getting him is over my dead body."

"Mine too!" Audrey shouted.

Mr. Fairfield seemed about to say something, but then a bold kid named Ryan Lund darted out of the class group. "Hey!" Sheriff Grimes snapped, to no effect: Ryan ran right over and stood next to Martin and Audrey. "Yeah, mine too!" He showed no fear at all of Rufus—who tensed up for a second, but then, apparently sensing that Ryan was more friend than foe, turned away.

Now Kaitlin Mallory broke away from the group and ran over next to Ryan. "Mine too!"

What happened next left everybody over the age of twelve all but speechless. First it was Jared Muller, then Emily Sprowl. Then Mia Costello. One by one, the seventh graders sprang past the policemen and ran over to stand with the others in front of Rufus. "Me too!" "Same here!" "Mine too!" they shouted, one after the other, as they parked themselves in Ben Fairfield's line of fire. Soon the whole class was on its way over to join the group.

Sheriff Grimes and his deputies tried to stop them. "Hey! . . . Hold it there. . . . No, you kids are going *inside,* you understand?" They managed to catch a few of them, but it wasn't nearly enough to stop the wave of young bodies surging past them. Finally, a bewildered-looking Donald Grimes was the only one left standing where the rest of the class had just been.

The sheriff's face was scarlet. "All right," he bellowed, "when I say three, you will all step away from there and go inside the building. One— Donnie! What are you doing?" He looked totally aghast as his own son slipped around him and headed over to join the others.

"Sorry, Dad," said Donald—being careful not to get *too* close to Rufus. "Sometimes you gotta go with the flow." Rufus, clearly recognizing him, shot a glower his way and growled. "Yeesh," Donald rasped, cringing, and took one more step away.

The sheriff just stood there with his mouth hanging open. Mr. Fairfield rolled his eyes, and the rest of the men looked lost. Nobody seemed to know what to do next—including Martin.

He glanced over at the school building, where Mrs.

Sanders, Principal Clayborne, and some other teachers were struggling to keep a mob of kids from the other classes from pouring onto the field. *This could get out of control,* he thought.

Suddenly, there were three quick *thunks* that startled Rufus, and he reared back, letting out a piercing ROAR that echoed halfway across town. It made everybody flinch, and the kids around him shuffled and murmured nervously.

"Shhh, okay, okay," said Martin, placing a calming hand on the big creature's side.

The sound, he realized, was car doors slamming. Everybody looked over to see three people working their way through the small crowd that was starting to gather outside the gate at the far side of the field, held there by a lone deputy. At first Martin had no idea who they were, but when he noticed Audrey's face light up, he recognized one of them.

"Mr. Eckhart!" she called.

Martin had pretty much forgotten about him ever since their downtown scramble. But here he was, accompanied by a tall, thin woman with thick glasses and an older gentleman who looked very distinguished in his charcoal-gray business suit.

Mr. Eckhart exchanged a few words with the officer, who allowed the three of them to pass through.

"Sweet Mother McGreevy!" said the tall woman breathlessly as they approached. "Am I dreaming?"

"Will you look at that!" said the man in the suit. "You weren't lying, Peter. Well done!"

"Thanks," said Mr. Eckhart. "I think."

"This is beyond everything in all the history of . . . everything!" the thin woman said. "And those kids! Shouldn't you be afraid?"

The schoolkids shrugged and mumbled, as though they hadn't really thought about it that much.

"I never thought I'd live to see it," the older man said. "Peter, you have made an amazing, amazing find."

"Not me, actually," said Mr. Eckhart. "Those two." He pointed to Audrey and Martin. Martin felt as though a beam of light were shooting straight from that finger to his chest, and it tingled through his body.

"Uh, excuse me," Ben Fairfield chimed in gruffly. "Who are you people?"

Mr. Eckhart gave an embarrassed smile. "Oh, sorry. You're Mr. Fairfield from the Trout Palace, aren't you?"

Ben nodded.

"I'm Peter Eckhart, the kids' science teacher. This is—"

"Ohhh. So *you're* Eckhart."

"Um . . . yes?" He looked a bit lost for a moment. "Guess my reputation precedes me. Anyway, this is Dr. Sydney Mahler, chairman of the zoology department at the U."

Dr. Mahler reached her hand out to Mr. Fairfield, but never took her eyes off Rufus. "Pleasure."

"Brantford Eliot, university president," said the

older man, also shaking Ben's hand. "Looks to me like you folks have been having a bit of an adventure here."

"You got that right," said Sheriff Grimes sharply, as if hoping to remind everyone who was the official authority on the scene.

"Well, I can't say I blame you," said Dr. Eliot, beaming. "This is absolutely extraordinary!"

Dr. Mahler was still awed by the sight of Rufus surrounded by all those seventh graders. "Why isn't somebody getting eaten?"

"That's what *I'd* like to know," said the sheriff brusquely.

Martin's classmates laughed. "He's not really that dangerous," said Audrey. Martin threw her a vaguely doubtful look. "I mean usually," she said. "If you treat him well."

Dr. Mahler edged her way over and stood among the kids, daring to gently touch Rufus's coarse skin. Martin was about to tell her that wasn't such a great idea, but Rufus was quite a bit calmer now, and didn't seem to mind.

"Sorry it took me so long to get back here, guys," Mr. Eckhart said to Martin and Audrey. "There was a bit of convincing to do."

"How did you find us?" Martin said.

"Not too hard. Just followed the crowd. I hope I'm not too late."

Martin wasn't quite sure how to answer that. "Well . . ." Knowing his dad would be chiming in at any time, he looked over at him with a sullen frown.

Mr. Eckhart saw the look and stepped over to Martin's parents.

"Mr. and Mrs. Tinker, I presume?"

"That's right," said Mr. Tinker flatly.

"Guess you're the ones to talk to," said Mr. Eckhart with an awkward chuckle. "Um . . . well, here's the thing. I talked this whole business over . . . I mean we talked it over, Syd and I—uh, Dr. Mahler—we discussed it with Dr. Eliot and, um . . . well, the whole board of regents, actually—"

"Oh, let me do it," said Dr. Eliot, stepping in front of him. "Sir, you're the current custodian of that magnificent creature, is that right?"

Mr. Tinker nodded.

Ben Fairfield lowered the tranquilizing gun. "Uh, actually—"

"Here's what we can propose," Dr. Eliot continued. "Our school has an academic exchange program with the University of Mérida in Mexico. And *they* have a five-hundred-acre plot of virgin rain forest in the Yucatán Peninsula that they let us use for research. Zoology, botany, what have you. Long story short, we feel it would be a perfect situation to move His Majesty permanently to the preserve."

"The idea being," said Dr. Mahler, "to study him in the closest thing to his natural environment."

Mr. Fairfield jumped in. "Yeah, well, here's the thing. You're gonna have to—"

"Hold on just a minute, Ben," Mr. Tinker said. "Let's let the man talk, okay?"

Ben Fairfield looked dumbfounded. He wasn't used to being shushed.

"Yes, yes, I know," said Dr. Eliot. "No doubt you're concerned about remuneration. I completely understand. I wish I could say here's a check for gazillions. Unfortunately, the university charter doesn't allow outlays for this type of thing."

Mr. Tinker nodded slowly, giving no hint of what he was thinking. Even Martin couldn't get a read on it.

"Now, it's possible we can find a way to work around that," said Dr. Eliot, "but I can make no guarantees. That's the long and, I daresay, short of it."

Mr. Eckhart spoke up. "It would certainly be the most humane situation for . . . um . . ."

"Rufus," Martin and Audrey said at the same time.

Mr. and Mrs. Tinker remained silent. Martin kept staring at them, trying to figure out what they could possibly be thinking.

The silence was broken by Ben Fairfield's gravelly voice. "Yeah, this is all well and good, folks, but unfortunately you're talking to the wrong guy. These people have already made a financial arrangement with me for disposition of the beast. So, thanks for the thought, but no thanks. Right, Gordo?"

He tried to give a chummy grin to Martin's dad, though he had to really work at it. Mr. Tinker squirmed a bit, let out a long breath, and gave a nervous cough. "Uhhh . . ." Everybody was still looking at him, which certainly wasn't helping him think about it rationally.

Martin had never seen him so twitchy. Though

he was still pretty angry, it occurred to him that it probably wasn't so easy being in his dad's shoes either.

Finally, Mr. Tinker spoke. "'Scuse us a sec."

He took Mrs. Tinker aside, and the two of them whispered back and forth. It went on for a good minute or so, until Mr. Fairfield's fake smile turned into an impatient glare. *"Gordo."*

Martin's dad looked at Ben sullenly, then turned to Dr. Eliot. "Your idea sounds okay, Professor," he said quietly. "The thing is, my wife and I aren't really in a position to give you an answer one way or the other. You're going to have to talk to the owner of the dinosaur."

Martin went rigid as his dad looked over at Ben Fairfield. "That's him right there."

Martin bit down hard, his fingernails digging into his palms, as the beginnings of a self-satisfied smirk appeared at the corners of Mr. Fairfield's mouth. But before it made it all the way to a smile, Mr. Tinker's left index finger went up in the air and snapped straight out—pointing directly at Martin.

In an instant, all the fire within Martin seemed to evaporate. Could this be? He felt the heavy knot in his throat loosen.

Audrey broke out in a huge smile, and so did most of their classmates. Some chuckled or whispered. A few applauded. Even Rufus seemed to perk up.

"Aha," said Dr. Eliot, turning his attention to Martin. "So that would be you, sir?"

"Whoa, whoa, whoa, hold the phone, here," Ben Fairfield interjected loudly. "Gordon, I believe your memory is failing you. We made a deal. You shook my hand, and you took my deposit. *Remember?*"

"Uh, yeah, about that," said Mr. Tinker. "I don't think so." He took Fairfield's check out of his shirt pocket and held it out to him. Ben took a step back as though it were on fire.

"What do you mean, you don't think so? A deal is a deal! Frank, you were there. Tell him!"

Sheriff Grimes seemed a bit surprised to be brought into it. "Uh, well . . . actually, Ben, I'm not sure exactly what the law says on that one. I think he has to actually cash it, or there has to be a written thing, or . . . I dunno. It's a civil deal. Not my domain, eh?"

Some of the seventh graders laughed at this, but Mr. Fairfield's face only got redder. "Don't be a moron, Tinker! I'm offering you a big fat revenue stream for *life*. You want to throw away millions?"

"Ben, if it wasn't for Martin, there'd be no dinosaur," Mr. Tinker said calmly. "I'd say we owe him a fair shake out of this, wouldn't you?"

"All right, all right! You wanna play hardball? I'll double the advance, *plus* the split on revenue."

Mr. Tinker said nothing.

"Fine!" Mr. Fairfield snapped. "We'll rejigger the split. Fifty-five you, forty-five me."

Martin's dad gave a tiny snicker and shook his head, as though finally getting a joke he had heard some time ago.

"Sixty-forty!" Ben shouted. "Look, friend, this is not a good way to start a business relationship!"

Mr. Tinker looked at him coolly. "Ben, you just finished calling me a moron. You slugged a defenseless animal with a stick, you insulted my wife, and you pointed a weapon at my son. Can you give me one good reason why I would want to be in a business relationship with you?"

With perfect timing, Rufus made a hacking sound that sounded almost like a laugh—and the surrounding kids picked up on it and had a good laugh of their own.

Ben Fairfield was not laughing. Spewing a string of unrepeatables, he flung the dart gun to the ground and spun away from the others.

"Ben, really," said Mrs. Tinker. "There are kids here."

Mr. Eckhart stepped over to Martin. "So what do you think, Martin? Yucatán?"

Martin felt everybody's eyes on him, and it made him a little nervous. This was a decision he'd been desperately hoping he could make, but now that he was being asked to actually make it, he was feeling a heavy weight of responsibility.

"You asked me to find a good place for him," Mr. Eckhart went on. "I'd say this is pretty good."

"Will he be happy there?"

"Can't say for sure, but—"

"A lot happier than he'd be around here," Dr. Mahler

interjected, while running her hand lightly over Rufus's upper back.

"Especially when December rolls around," Mr. Eckhart added with a smile.

Suddenly, Rufus gave a testy snort and snapped at Dr. Mahler—who jumped away in a flash. "Hoh! Okay, moving on . . ."

The kids hopped back too, and the policemen reached for their guns.

"No, it's okay!" Martin shouted. "He's okay! He's just a little crowded." He petted Rufus gently on the curve of his lower back. "We're okay," he said quietly. "Right, boy? Everything's good."

Rufus calmed down immediately. But Martin couldn't escape the thought that his big friend, this closest pal he'd ever had, was no longer the playful little lizard he had kept hidden in the barn.

He exchanged a rueful look with Audrey. He knew she was thinking the same thing he was.

She turned to Mr. Eckhart. "Can we visit him?"

Dr. Mahler and Mr. Eckhart both looked to Dr. Eliot, and he gave a grandfatherly grin. "I don't see why not."

Martin looked at Rufus, who lowered his head to sniff at a patch of dandelions.

"So?" said Mr. Eckhart. "What's the verdict?"

Martin felt like there was one more thing he had to do before saying anything else. "Just a sec." He leaned over, gently put his hand on Rufus's neck, and whispered something in his reptilian ear cavity. Rufus stood still, as though he was actually listening— although it might have just been a busy anthill down there that was holding his attention. Then, all of a sudden, his head jerked up and he lurched forward with a loud explosion of air shooting from his nostrils—a jumbo Jurassic sneeze that made everybody jump.

"He says yes," Martin said, and everyone laughed. Mr. Eckhart reached out his hand, and as Martin shook it, he felt that giant weight of responsibility being lifted away, and he broke into his first real smile in what seemed like days.

Now a wave of curious energy swept through the crowd of kids. They pressed in around Martin and Audrey and started peppering them with questions. "Where did you guys get him?" "Where did you keep him?" "What does he eat?" "Can I touch him?" Martin and Audrey did their best to answer, but the questions came so fast that they couldn't keep up. For now, though, Martin was perfectly content just to bask in the sunlight of his new and strange role of star of the seventh grade.

Ben Fairfield was still steaming. "Last chance, Gordon. You can honor our deal or be a big loser for the rest of your life. Which is it gonna be?"

Mr. Tinker looked unruffled. "Guess it's gonna be loser."

"You got it, pal. You are fired!"

"Thank you, Ben," said Martin's dad. "Saves me

having to tell you to take a long hike off a short pier." Mrs. Tinker faked a cough to cover up a snicker.

"Yeah, that's real funny. Hey, I've got a good one: that's not the end of this. Come on," Ben said to Jasper and Ollie as he marched away. When he noticed they weren't following him, he turned and gave them a look that could torch an iceberg. That got them going, and they followed him across the field and out the gate.

Martin saw his dad hold up Ben's check, scrutinizing it with a look of nagging doubt, and maybe even some regret. "Hey, we'll be okay," Mrs. Tinker reassured him. "It'll work out." She leaned her forehead on his shoulder and reached her arms around him, squeezing hard.

Sheriff Grimes and his officers just stood there, looking like they weren't quite sure what they were supposed to do at this point. They kept an eye on Rufus, but he didn't seem like that much of a danger now.

To Martin, it seemed like Rufus was actually enjoying all the attention—which was exactly how he was feeling himself. Though he knew he would soon have to say good-bye to his prehistoric friend, for now he was perfectly happy to answer questions and show off his unusual pet to his classmates and the professors. (And yes—now a lopsided grin had even found its way onto Donald's unruly face.)

Over at the field entrance, the police officer allowed a small swarm of news reporters with their camera crews through the gate, and they rushed on the scene and started chattering away—though keeping a safe distance from Rufus. Then a man's voice rose up above the general din.

"Audrey!"

J.B. and Jade Blanchard pushed past the reporters and ran toward the kids and Rufus.

"Daddy!" Audrey shouted, running straight into a giant bear hug with her dad and sister—who couldn't seem to decide whether to be more thrilled to find that Audrey was okay, or more astonished to see Rufus and his posse of young admirers.

Martin smiled wistfully at the sight of the Blanchards huddled together. Then he looked again at his parents, standing hand in hand while calmly watching the strange scene taking place around the tall T. rex, just a few short strides in front of them. He locked gazes with his dad, who threw him a crooked little smile and a wink.

If you didn't know the Tinkers, you might not think much about that wink. But it was something Martin hadn't seen from his dad in a long, long time, and he didn't have to catch a football to earn it.

# EPILOGUE

ONE WEEK LATER

The sun beat down like a giant flamethrower, and the air was thick with humidity. That was nothing unusual in this part of the world, but it sure felt alien to Martin as he strode slowly across the grassy clearing. Rufus lumbered along next to him, and Audrey kept pace on the other side. When the three of them got to the edge of the clearing, they stopped, looking into the dense, forbidding thicket of trees just a few steps ahead.

A lot of questions suddenly popped into Martin's head, but when he turned around to ask, he saw that the people who might answer were not right behind him, as he had thought, but were standing in a group on the other side of the clearing. Mr. and Mrs. Tinker, J.B. and Jade Blanchard, Mr. Eckhart,

Dr. Mahler, and a few other professors and scientists were waiting patiently. When Jade raised her phone and started snapping photos, Martin knew this was meant as a moment for himself and Audrey, and no one else.

He looked over at Audrey with an uncertain expression, and she looked back with a strained grin, though her eyes looked sadder than he had ever seen them. It made him aware of the lump in his own throat, and he tried hard to swallow it.

He looked up at Rufus. "Don't worry, boy," he said, barely above a whisper. "We won't forget you."

Rufus seemed a bit disoriented. Who could blame him? He'd been shipped in a special cage on a special plane, then hauled in a special truck on a bumpy dirt road . . . and now here he was, in a strange new place. This plainly was not Menominee Springs. Yet there was something about the forest in front of him that seemed to intrigue him.

Martin and Audrey both came at him at once, one on each side, awkwardly delivering heartfelt hugs to his hug-resistant frame.

"This is your home now," said Martin. "It's time for you to go. Go on."

Rufus's dark eyes scanned the wall of trees, as though trying to decide what to make of it. He twitched and snorted, then looked down at Martin and Audrey.

"Go, Rufus!" Audrey said.

Rufus took one more look at the jungle, then threw his head back and let out a mighty ROAR that echoed through the trees. Bobbing his head once, he took a slow step forward, then another, and then another.

"Bye, Rufus!" Audrey called. "Be good!"

"G'bye, boy!" Martin shouted. "We'll come visit, we promise!"

The closer Rufus got to the forest, the heavier Martin's heart became. He couldn't help thinking of Orville the hamster, and now that same feeling of stinging loss was hitting him again. But it wasn't exactly the same, because he knew Rufus was still there, and he was probably going to do just fine. It was the end of the best time of Martin's life . . . but maybe the beginning of something even better.

Everybody watched as Rufus reached the edge of the forest and took a careful step into the brush. A few jungle birds were sounding the alarm, but all the humans stayed perfectly still and quiet. Martin glanced back at his parents, and he could tell from their faces that even they were feeling a little sad.

Rufus pushed his way slowly in among the trees, moving forward step by hesitant step, and soon all anybody could see in the foliage was a single patch of grayish-brown skin on his back. Audrey couldn't hold back a fluttery sniff, and Martin tried another swallow against that stubborn lump.

The scaly patch faded and shrank as the big creature ambled farther into the hazy greenery.

Then the patch disappeared, but Martin could still make out the very tip of Rufus's tail, flicking lightly against a wide, drooping leaf.

And then, in an instant . . . he was gone.

The two of them stood there staring into the forest, trying to compose themselves before heading back to join the others. They both took a deep breath and, at exactly the same time, exhaled with a quiet, rueful sigh.

"Holy mama . . . ," she said.

"Ai-yai-yai . . . ," he said.

They looked at each other and laughed a little, which helped break the sadness of the moment. Then, as they looked back at the forest one more time, Martin felt a strange sensation in the palm of his left hand, something warm and soft and almost jarringly unfamiliar. It took him a couple of seconds to realize it was Audrey's hand, grasping his.

It was nothing at all like a spear or a football or a bug net. It felt nice.

# 10 THINGS TO KNOW ABOUT DINOSAURS

1. An adult T. REX was more than 40 feet long, weighed 7 tons, had 6-inch-long teeth, and could swallow 500 pounds of meat in one bite. No other dinosaurs ever made fun of T. rex.

2. Though STEGOSAURUS was as big as an elephant, its brain was the size of a kumquat. It also wandered around eating plants all day. So what did it need a brain for, really?

3. ORNITHOMIMUS could run over 40 miles per hour. In a footrace with Usain Bolt, it would eat his lunch. Then it would eat him.

4. Of the more than 900 species of dinosaurs that have been discovered, over 100 were found in Great Britain. Scientists have determined that these dinosaurs enjoyed tea and crumpets and walked on the left side of the migration path.

5. The largest known winged dinosaur, QUETZALCOATLUS, had a wingspan of up to 40 feet—as big as an airplane. There is no evidence, however, that they had retracting wheels or overhead storage bins.

6. Based on brain size relative to body size, TROODONS are considered to have been the smartest dinosaurs. They almost always won on *Paleo Jeopardy*.

7. The biggest dinosaur discovered so far is DREADNOUGHTUS—an 85-foot-long plant eater that weighed as much as 77 tons. Even T. rex probably didn't bother trying to chow down on that one—it would be like a human trying to take a bite out of a 900-pound cheeseburger with a gigantic swinging tail.

8. The smallest known dinosaur, ANCHIORNIS, was about the size of a robin and was covered with feathers. In fact, a lot of dinosaurs had feathers. But they never figured out how to make a duster or a pillow.

9. Some dinosaurs had big hollow crests on their skulls, which may have helped them trumpet loudly to attract a mate. Some of their favorite songs to sing were "I'm Just a Big Lonely Lizard," "Look So Fine, My Six-Ton Valentine," and "Let's Get Together Before We All Go Extinct."

10. Contrary to common belief (and the previous sentence), dinosaurs did not really go extinct 65 million years ago; they evolved into birds and still live with us today. So, yes: hummingbirds, penguins, ostriches, turkeys, your pet parakeet, Big Bird, the Aflac duck—dinos all. Consider THAT the next time you sit down for Thanksgiving dinner. . . .

# ACKNOWLEDGMENTS

No doubt there are writers who can take a rough pebble, retreat into a dim cubby, exclude the rest of humanity from their process, and emerge some weeks or months later with a perfectly polished pearl. I'm not one of them.

Robert Newcombe, your contributions in turning an idle thought into a real thing on paper were invaluable. My unending thanks.

To the early road-testers of the first tentative fragments—Dan and Harrison Hirsch, Emily and Dominic Fulk, Marcia Midkiff, Steve Sprung—I am grateful. Here's the rest of it for you.

Dave LeLacheur and the whole LeLacheur clan (Sam and Gwen, you're still the first!), your feedback and moral support have been golden. Many, many thanks.

To the "Greenline" critique group—Jennifer Mann, Leslie Caulfield, Shari Becker—my gratitude.

Michelle Poploff, editor extraordinaire: a giant THANK YOU for adopting this bad boy and expertly guiding it to the finish line. You'll be my hero for the duration.

And Krista Vitola, your insights and positive energy have been a perfect finishing touch, and I appreciate it.

It's been a grand journey. I'm glad you were all a part of it.

## ABOUT THE AUTHOR

DAVID FULK is an award-winning playwright, screenwriter and director, and novelist. One of six children, he grew up near Chicago and has lived in Missouri, Louisiana, Michigan, California, Pennsylvania, New York, Texas, Belgium, India, and (yes) Wisconsin. He currently lives near Boston with his pet T. rex, Rosie.